The Naval Knaves

A New Sherlock Holmes Mystery

Note to Readers:

Your enjoyment of this new Sherlock Holmes mystery will be enhanced by re-reading the original story that inspired this one —
The Naval Treaty.
It has been appended and may be found in the back portion of this book.

The Naval Knaves

A New Sherlock Holmes Mystery

Craig Stephen Copland

Published by:

Conservative Growth

1101 30th Street NW, Ste. 500

Washington, DC 20007

Cover design by Rita Toews

ISBN-10:   1973908077

ISBN-13:   978-1973908074

Dedication

While writing this story, the Canadian media has been full of stories of forest fires in British Columbia and the courageous men and women who are fighting them around the clock. To them I dedicate this book. The story has nothing whatsoever to do with fighting wildfires, except that a few days after it is published, we're moving to BC. So, I want those brave fire fighters to know how much I appreciate them.

Contents

Acknowledgements

All writers of Sherlock Holmes fan fiction or pastiche stories are indebted to the genius of Sir Arthur Conan Doyle or, for the true Sherlockians, to Dr. John Watson, for the creation of the sixty original stories, the Canon, of Sherlock Holmes.

In this story, I also borrow from Henry James. He is not my favorite author but he wrote a great book about a beautiful anarchist.

My dearest and closest friend, Mary Engelking, not only encourages the continued writing of these stories but proofreads, edits, and point out places where I was incoherent.

Several wonderful and invaluable fans of Sherlock Holmes have kindly offered their services as Beta readers and provided exceptionally worthwhile comments, suggestions, and corrections. I extend my gratitude to them yet again.

It has been a while since I acknowledged my high school English teachers at Scarlett Height Collegiate Institute in Toronto — Bill Stratton, Norm Oliver, and Margaret Tough — who inspired me to read and write. I am deeply indebted to them.

Chapter One
A Diplomatic Problem

Seven years ago, in the year of Our Lord 1887, Great Britain and Italy entered into a secret agreement that both countries expected would help them accomplish their colonial ambitions in the Mediterranean, and frustrate those of Russia and France. It was that treaty which was stolen from the office of my dear school chum, Percy Phelps, and nearly sold into the wrong foreign hands. Had it not been for the brilliant detective work of Sherlock Holmes, a serious international incident could have arisen and who knows what terrible events might subsequently have taken place. I put an account of these events on paper in the story I called *The Naval Treaty,* but I withheld publication for a few years until I thought that the possibility of any dangerous repercussions had passed.

How wrong I was.

In the years since that adventure, all sorts of tumultuous international intrigues have occurred. Agreements and promises between nations have been made and broken. Germany entered into a Re-Insurance Treaty with Russia, only to fail to renew it two years later. Italy joined with Germany and Austro-Hungary and formed what would come to be known as the Triple Alliance. Russia and France became quite cozy with each other. The Ottomans, while a mere shadow of the great empire of the past, remained unpredictable and prickly.

Africa, that great dark continent, was the victim of the relentless pursuit of colonial claims upon its people and territories. Great Britain and France led the scramble, but Belgium, Portugal, Germany, Spain, and Italy also grabbed pieces of property. The British had a dream of a great north-south red line of our colonies stretching from the Cape to Cairo. The French envisioned an east-west line of their territories from Senegal to Djibouti. Any school boy with a starter's knowledge of geometry could predict that those two lines would have to intersect somewhere, sometime, and one of them would have to become intermittent.

Skirmishes and minor conflicts between nations were inevitable. Much more common was the omnipresence of spies and double agents, clandestine skulduggery, and unending machinations, plots, and espionage. Some of these efforts involved the stealing of state secrets. Some involved murder. So, it was only a matter of time before the unique skills of Sherlock Holmes would be called upon yet again to help the individuals caught in the webs of intrigue and, indeed, to help the Empire itself.

This particular intriguing adventure that I am about to recount to you began pleasantly enough on a morning in late August. My dear wife Mary (née Morstan) and I were enjoying a cup of tea and a chat together when the daily post arrived.

"Oh, darling," she said, "will you look at this?"

"What is it, my love?"

"Quite the official letter from the Admiralty. It's addressed to both of us. Mind if I open it?"

"Go right ahead, dear. It must be from Percy; we certainly do not know anyone else there."

Percy Phelps had recovered from the traumatic time when he was under suspicion for the theft of the 1887 treaty and had gone on to do highly commendable work in the Foreign Office. In the fall of 1891, a coveted billet in the Admiralty opened up. With some assistance from his uncle, who was then serving as both the Prime Minister and the Foreign Secretary, Percy won the appointment and became the Senior Assistant to Sir Ughtred Kay-Shuttleworth, the Parliamentary Secretary to the Admiralty. The timing was most fortunate, as the Conservatives narrowly went down to defeat in 1892 and the Liberals came into power. Percy, by dint of his diligence and brilliance, retained his post and proved himself an invaluable aid to the powers that be, regardless of their party. His life appeared to be on a gilded trajectory, and there was talk bruited about that a position in the Cabinet might someday be offered to him.

"Oo la la," cooed Mary as she read the gilt-edged notice. "We have been invited to a reception for the Secretary of the Navy of *La République de France*; to be held at the Langham Hotel on the fifteenth of September. Oh, John, darling, you have become such a famous author that we are mingling with the bluebloods."

I smiled warmly back at her. "That is very kind of you to suggest that our invitation is a result of my stories about Sherlock, but you and I know perfectly well that your dear friend, Annie Phelps, was behind this invitation and the reason is that she has no interest in having to go to yet another swank affair with Percy only to have him abandon her whilst he runs around playing host and major domo."

"Oh, perhaps that might have had something to do with it, but all those stuffed shirts and feathered ladies love your stories. Do you suppose that Sherlock was sent an invitation as well?"

"I'm quite sure he was."

"Do you think he will attend?"

"I'm quite sure he will not. He loathes pretension of all types and such behavior will be on display in spades. I feel somewhat the same way myself."

I could see immediately in the vanishing of her smile that my comment was not a wise thing to say.

"But John, darling, you look so dashing and handsome when all in formal dress. I love being on the arm of such a famous author and gentleman."

I sighed inwardly. We were going to the diplomatic event. I thought that all I would have to do would be to chat amiably with Annie Phelps while her husband was occupied with official duties, and grin and bear the rest of the evening.

I had maintained my friendship with Percy, and we met from time to time in his club to reminisce and chat. He was deeply grateful for the help I had given in bringing Sherlock Holmes into his life and was keen to keep up a warm and continuing friendship. Much more than that, however, was the intimate friendship that had formed and grown between his wife, Annie (née Harrison) and Mary. They met at the Phelps-Harrison wedding, to which Holmes and I had been invited. They hit it off and for several years had met regularly for tea when Annie came up from Woking to London.

Mrs. Phelps, in addition to being a good friend to my wife, was wonderfully devoted to her husband and the two of them seemed to be perfectly happy with their lot in life. All in all, the life of Percy Phelps and those in his immediate circle, could not have been going better. He was involved in a hive of activities that had implications for the continuing prosperity of the Empire, and he was loving every minute of it. Truly, these were his halcyon days. Being the decent, good-hearted fellow that he was, he followed the advice to all young men on the rise; *be good to those who help you on the way up, because you may meet them again on your way back down.* Thus, he brought over to the Admiralty with him Mr. Charles Gorot, the brilliant clerk who now served as his secretary, as well as

5

Mr. and Mrs. Tangay and their daughter to provide service in the suite of offices. All three of the Tangay family were given new, starched uniforms, replete with a few brass buttons and short pieces of gold braid, as was befitting anyone who worked at the Admiralty. They were ferociously loyal to Queen and country, and they could not have been more plumped and proud.

The fifteenth of September began as a pleasant autumn day, sunny and cool, but the rain held off and the temperature in the evening hovered just above the fifty-degree mark. Our primary duty at the reception was to look after Mrs. Phelps whilst Percy was busy. She had no intention of being abandoned and left to fend for herself, a beautiful but common girl from Northumberland amongst the well-coiffed, elegant vipers of Belgravia.

The reception, which began at four o'clock, was in honor of the Naval Minister of France, Monsieur Auguste Alfred Lefèvre. He and his entourage had arrived in England for a series of meetings with his counterparts in the Cabinet and the Admiralty. All sorts of Lord So-and-So and Lady Such-and-Such were present and dressed to the nines. It was expected that a member of the Royal family would make an appearance.

The Langham, one of the very select hotels of London, was elegantly adorned with tri-color bunting and the flags of the two nations hanging side-by-side. The hotel staff were dutifully attentive, constantly offering Champagne or other social lubricants to the over two-hundred guests. The hotel staff were augmented by a few of the service people from the

Admiralty, in their starched, buttoned, and gold-braided uniforms. It was one of those splendid affairs where everyone engaged in intimate conversation whilst at the same time looking over the shoulder of the person they were talking to in order to see if someone more important had arrived.

The French, of course, were everywhere. Their Ambassador and his staff, several wealthy French business owners, and no end of dashing gentlemen in military uniforms, with sashes, swords, medals, and epaulettes were strutting and bowing and doing all those things that the French do so well, and make them so annoying, as they seek to establish their superior *savoir-faire* to the all-too-gauche English.

At just after five o'clock, when the room was filled with guests and all abuzz with bantering inconsequence, the tall, lean Charles Gorot approached the three of us, accompanied by two gentlemen and a young lady.

"Ah, Dr. and Mrs. Watson and Mrs. Phelps," said Charles, "allow me to introduce our honored guests from the Continent."

I concluded that Percy had given him orders to bring interesting people to us so that Mrs. Phelps would be entertained and engaged, as there was no other reason that distinguished foreign guests would want to talk to common folk like us.

"Dr. Watson," Charles continued, "is the famous author of the stories of the great detective, Sherlock Holmes. The Admiralty had invited Mr. Holmes as well, but he was entirely too busy solving a terrible crime to attend."

Charles gave a sly wink to the three of us and smiled at Annie, who beamed a warm smile back at him.

"Allow me," Charles said, "to present the lovely Princess Casamassima of the State of Aosta in Italy. She is the guest of Captain François l'Olannais and Captain August Duhaut-Cilly, who I am also honored to introduce to you. They have been visiting us in the Admiralty for the past several months and helping us to prepare for the evening's announcement of splendid cooperation between our two great nations."

Being French, they both bowed gallantly. I had to admit that in their full-dress French navy uniforms they were handsome, bordering on breathtaking. They were both tall and broad-shouldered, with wavy, black hair, trim mustaches, and aristocratic faces that could have been sculpted out of marble.

If the young woman's appearance could be summed up in one word, it would be dazzling. She was fair and slender. Her beauty had a character of perfection; it astonished. Her dark eyes, between blue and gray, were as intoxicating as they were lovely, and there was an extraordinary light nobleness in the way she held her head. Two or three diamond stars glittered in the thick, delicate hair. A radiance of youth and eminence and success shone from her face.

"Princess, this is indeed an honor," I said as I bowed and accepted the elegant, alabaster, bejeweled hand. "And Captains," I added and gave a head bob of a bow in their direction. "I do hope that you are not missing the charms of France and Italy too much and that you are enjoying such sights and adventures as we can offer here in England."

"Why, thank you, doctor," replied the princess. "we are being very well-treated but, of course, what we have fallen in love with is your glorious English weather." She smiled a wide, perfect smile.

Her voice had the lilt of coquettish sarcasm, and the entire lot of us broke out into laughter. What surprised me, however, was that she had not a trace of an Italian accent.

"Good heavens!" exclaimed Annie Phelps. "You're an American."

Annie was from the far north of England, that county that lies along the border. Beyond it is what most Englishmen call *terra incognito* but which appears on maps as Scotland. Like a true Northumbrian, she valued plain-speaking highly and diplomatic niceties not at all. For a second, I panicked at the *faux pas,* but the Princess laughed and graciously replied.

"Well, hey there, honey child, nobody's perfect. But I will have you know that I am a true blue-blood. Why, I come from the Blue Ridge Mountains." We all laughed along with her.

Over the next fifteen minutes, we engaged in enjoyable conversation as I questioned our guests concerning their sojourn in England. The French Captains gave several Gallic shrugs and condescending smiles and regretted their need for discretion. They could only say that they were involved in diplomatic discussions that would be of mutual benefit to the navies of both countries.

The beautiful Princess Casamassima was exceptionally composed and explained that she was conducting a study across Europe regarding the condition of the poor and the efforts made for their upliftment by the governments of the

European states.

Our chat was ended when an official from the Admiralty called the room to order and requested that we all be seated. Charles, with a warm smile to Annie and Mary, excused himself and ushered the princess and the captains to their reserved seats at the front whilst the three of us found a place to sit near the back of the hall.

The formal program began, and we all stood as Prince Alfred, the son of the Queen and the Commander of the Mediterranean Fleet, ascended to the dais. He started into some high-sounding remarks as might be expected on the occasion. He was a fine speaker, but my attention was distracted.

Standing in the doorway of the hall, just behind us, was the unmistakable figure of Inspector Lestrade of Scotland Yard. Surely, I thought, there was no need for additional police presence at this event. The Welsh Guards were stationed throughout, every one of them carrying his sword and several of them bearing real rifles and girdled with full ammunition belts.

Out of the corner of my eye, I watched as Lestrade whispered silently with one of the hotel staff, who pointed him toward Percy Phelps. As unobtrusively as he could, the inspector hunched over and walked up the aisle to where Percy was sitting and tapped him on the shoulder. Percy was obviously not pleased with being so accosted. Doing so in the middle of the Prince's speech was an appalling violation of protocol. But Lestrade leaned over and whispered in his ear and Percy, looking quite alarmed, got up and walked back down the aisle to the door.

As he was passing, he saw me and gestured urgently that I should join them. I stumbled over several other guests and followed them into the lobby of the hall. Once the door had been closed behind us, Lestrade turned to me.

"Where's Holmes?"

I checked my watch.

"It is now a quarter to six on a Wednesday. I know he is still in England, and if he has not been called away from London on a case, he will be at home. He usually …"

"Let's go," interrupted Lestrade. "There are cabs lined up outside. Mr. Phelps, sir, could you please come with me. Dr. Watson, Forbes will join you."

"Mind if I let the ladies know what we are up to?" I asked.

"No time. They'll be fine," said Lestrade.

Without any further explanation, Lestrade walked quickly toward to front door of the hotel. Once there, he and Percy stepped into the first cab in the line, and I clambered up into the second one. I had met Inspector Forbes a few times in the past and immediately queried him.

"Inspector," I said, "can you tell me what this is all about?"

"Don't rightly know myself, doctor. All I know is that there was an incident in Greenwich, just by the Observatory, and it has the Yard perfectly spooked. It must be serious if Lestrade is calling in Sherlock Holmes right straight away. Beyond that, I'm as much in the dark as you are."

The Langham is only a few blocks from Baker Street, and we arrived at the door of 221B within ten minutes. I still had a key to the door on my key ring and let the four of us in. Percy Phelps and the two inspectors followed me up the stairs and into the familiar front room. Holmes was comfortably sitting there, clad in a dressing gown and holding his pipe in one hand and a book in the other. He at first looked pleasantly surprised to see me and then broke into a broad smile when the three other men entered the room.

"Percy! How grand to see you again but, oh my, this looks serious," he said, barely disguising the expectation in his voice. "Please, all of you, be seated. A brandy, perhaps?"

Chapter Two
Gut-Wrenching Anarchy

estrade ignored his offer. "Holmes, we have a problem."

"So it would appear. Do tell," said Holmes, sloping back in his chair and stretching his long legs out in front of him.

"There was an incident in Greenwich," said Lestrade. "At 4:50 this afternoon a couple of schoolboys were walking through the grounds of the Observatory. They hear an explosion, and not far from them they see a pillar of smoke rising. They run up to see what it's all about and they come on some poor bloke who is lying on the ground, his coat smoldering. He has his hand, or what's left of it, wrapped in his handkerchief and he's bleeding from it. But his jacket and sweater are also half blown away, and his stomach is all a bloody mess. So, the lads run like the devil and fetch the park attendants. They come running and the fellow, who is still alive and able to talk, says to call a cab to take him home. They say nothing doing and rush him over to the Seaman's Hospital where he lives for a bit longer, and then he dies."

Holmes had been puffing slowly on his pipe whilst listening to Lestrade's recitation. When the inspector paused, Holmes waited and looked at him with a puzzled look.

"My dear inspector," he said. "For the past decade, you have waited to call on my services until you knew that you were in far too deep to find a way out. Now you come here barely two hours after this incident. If this were only a case of another pathetic anarchist with a few sticks of dynamite, you would send your men out, track down all his network within a week and either have them behind bars or fleeing to America. Obviously, there is something more to this case, or you would not be here. Please elucidate."

"Right, Holmes. It weren't no ordinary run-of-the-mill anarchist. In this bloke's pocket, we found a detailed set of plans to the Greenwich Observatory. On it are a series of Xs showing where he was going to place his dynamite. If he had succeeded, he would have blown the Greenwich clocks to kingdom come. Those clocks send the time signals to every port all over the world, and not only our Fleet but the navies of our allies and the entire merchant marine depend on them. If they suddenly stopped there would be chaos on the high seas. Ships could be lost and flounder. All the shipping lanes of the globe would grind to a halt. It would be a financial disaster. The stock markets would crash."

"Ah, now that is interesting," said Holmes, "You have a visionary anarchist who is smart enough to do his homework beforehand, yet still stupid enough to blow his guts out. Wherein is the issue?"

"The issue, Holmes, is that those plans were secret. They were stamped with the seal of the Admiralty, and they are kept under lock and key in the vault. No one who is not authorized can ever get into them. But somehow, he got them. Are you understanding me now?"

"But you have them back, and he failed to do any damage."

"In the same vault are the plans for every British warship currently at sea, or has its keel already laid, or is planned. All of them. And the plans for all the major merchant ships, and every other large vessel registered in the Britain. That vault was penetrated. Are you getting this, Holmes?"

Holmes sat up in his chair and looked at Lestrade, Forbes, and Percy. Poor Percy was as pale as a sheet. Holmes turned to him.

"Percy, was your office responsible for the security of that vault?"

He made no reply. He closed his eyes and nodded his head.

"You will, I presume, report this immediately to Sir Ughtred and the Cabinet?"

Again, Percy nodded.

"And they," Holmes continued, "will report it to the Prime Minister?"

Another nod.

"A shame that he is a Liberal," said Holmes.

"'Tis," said four voices in unison.

"Very well, gentlemen," said Holmes. "I do not wish to make assumptions about your activities, but I assume that Scotland Yard will make an immediate list of all possible suspects, trace all their bank deposits and telegrams, talk to their neighbors, and winnow out the impossibles. Is that correct?"

"That's what we legal detectives have to do, Holmes," said Lestrade.

"And what then is it you wish me to do?"

"You know bloody well what we need you to do, Holmes. You need to do those things that we cannot because we are bound by the statutes and courts of this country. We have no idea who this dead bomber was and no record of him anywhere. You need to find out who he was and penetrate his network."

"Oh, is that all?"

"No. In the cab on the way over here, Mr. Phelps told me that he has two Frenchies who have been guests in his office for the past several months. Those two are at the top of my suspect list."

"Then arrest them," said Holmes.

"I cannot. They're diplomats. I cannot even make their time here difficult without having the French getting their *sooo vetements* in a knot and screaming about diplomatic immunity all the way from Paris."

"Ah, but you do not care if *I* were to that that."

"I do not care a flying fig, and furthermore I never said that, now did I, Holmes?"

"My dear inspector, I will immediately proceed to not working on anything, and will inform you of everything I never discover."

"Fine by me," said Lestrade.

"Well, then, gentlemen," said Holmes. "Allow me to bid you a good evening and return to your diplomatic *soirée*. I extend my sympathies to Dr. Watson and Mr. Phelps who will have to explain to their wives how it was that they were able to escape an evening of pomposity and pretension whilst the ladies had to endure it. Have a pleasant evening."

Holmes has an annoying habit of rubbing his hands when he is pleased with his prospects, and he was doing it again.

Percy and I returned to the Langham in time to find our wives standing at the door of the now nearly empty hall and looking not-in-the-least pleased or patient. I was sure they were going to take a strip off our hides, but the dark clouds on our faces silenced them.

We rode in silence back to our home and only after I had finished a full snifter of brandy did Mary broach the subject of the evening.

"Well, darling, are you going to tell me what happened, or is it all terribly secret?"

"No, dear. Some of it will be in the papers tomorrow, but the possible consequences are awfully frightening."

I then relayed all that I had heard and understood, and then I posed a question to her.

"Those French chaps, we had fifteen minutes with them, right?" I said.

"Yes, why?"

"What did you think of them? You know, your woman's intuition and all that."

"They are very impressive men. Wonderfully polished, suave, men of the world, and as handsome as a maiden could ever dream of."

"Darling," I said, "Even *I* could see all that. That's not what I asked you for."

"No? Very well, then, I suppose I could add that I would not trust those knaves as far as I could throw them, and neither would Annie."

"And would you like to tell me why?"

"No. I would not. And I would not because there is no *why*. There are only those things that a woman knows, and they cannot be explained rationally to a man, but they are never wrong."

Had I been a wiser man that I am, I would have left it at that, but I was not.

"My dear," I said. "That does not help me to understand. Come, now. What was it about them? What did they do that made you feel like that?"

She gave me a bit of a look before responding. "If you

must know, it was because I could see them, both of them, mentally undressing me in their minds until I was standing stark naked in front of them. That is why."

I knew I should not have asked.

I was certain that Holmes would be right on the case. Its combination of intrigue and importance would make it irresistible, and he would most likely go with little food or sleep, replaced by copious amounts of coffee and tobacco for however long it took to solve.

The next day, Thursday, passed and I heard nothing. By Friday afternoon, my curiosity had the better of me, and I walked over to Baker Street after finishing my appointments at my medical office. Mrs. Hudson greeted me at the door, warmly as always.

"Oh, Doctor, how lovely to see you. I am so sorry I missed you on Wednesday evening. I heard that you came charging in to Mr. Holmes along with the police. Well, you must have done something to him. He didn't come home at all last night and has just come back this past half hour. Shall I let him know you are here?"

Holmes was pacing back and forth and did not stop when I entered. He gestured me toward my familiar chair but remained on his feet.

"What ho, Holmes? Any news? Was it a worthy challenge?"

He said nothing and continued pacing, yet smiling ever so slightly. I waited.

Finally, "The initial stages of my investigation were

ridiculously easy. A first-year London bobby could have managed it. I can only assume that Lestrade assigned it to me so as not to announce to the *demi-monde* that Scotland Yard was investigating them. A complete abuse of my time and talents."

"Oh, come, come, you're still an Englishman and mustn't complain. So, what did you learn?"

"The schoolboys and park attendants who found the poor fool spoke to him before he was taken to hospital. They reported that he had a distinctly French accent. Had they said he was Irish, I would have been faced with a list of three dozen known dynamiters, every one of whom could have been inebriated enough to blow himself to pieces. But a Frenchman? That made it easier. All the French anarchists in London collude in the bowels of the Club Autonomie on Windmill Street in Fitzrovia. I went in disguise and soon learned that the dead man's name was Martial Bourdin. He is a radical tailor from Paris who has spent time both in a French prison and in America; which one was the greater punishment for his crimes is a matter of debate. He has been in London for the past year and associates constantly with his fellow anarchists. All that is left for Lestrade to do is raid the club and round up all of the members. And that will be that." He snapped his fingers for dramatic effect.

"But where did he get his dynamite?" I asked. "I thought that our government had restricted its purchase and use. And how did he know how to make a bomb?"

"Very good, Watson. Now, *those* are interesting questions. The second one is easily answered. In his pocket was a book borrowed from the British Museum Library. It gave detailed instructions on how to make a bomb. Unfortunately for Mr. Bourdin, it was in English, and it would appear that the chapter on how not to have your bomb explode when holding in your left hand against your stomach must have been lost in translation."

"Fine, but how in heaven's name did he have the plans for the inner working of the Observatory?"

"Brilliant, Watson! And it is to that question that I will now turn my attention, regardless of whether or not Lestrade wishes me too. The emerging web of intrigue is altogether too appealing to be left to the Yard."

His eyes were sparkling, and yet again he was rubbing his hands together.

He seemed so invigorated that I offered to propose a premature toast to the successful conclusion of this case.

"Not to the conclusion, Watson. To the chase. To the game." And so we toasted.

Our reverie was interrupted by the bell on Baker Street. Soon we were listening to a very slow set of footsteps climbing up toward us. They stopped part way up and then started again, slowly.

"An elderly and rather unhealthy man is coming to meet me," surmised Holmes. "I wonder who that could be."

The figure that entered the room was not at all elderly. It was Percy Phelps but, dear Lord, he was ghastly pale. His face was unshaven, and his clothes looked as if he had spent the past two days living in them. I had not seen him looking so near death since that sad day seven years ago when we visited him as he lay on his sick bed in Woking.

"Percy," I gasped and leapt to my feet. "Merciful heavens, my friend, what is it?"

He said nothing and walked slowly over to the settee and sat down. He tried to speak, but no words came forth. Tears appeared in his eyes and began to run down his cheeks. I reached for the decanter of brandy that was still open on the mantle and poured him a glass. He took a sip and then tipped the entire glass back and swallowed its contents.

"It's a disaster," he said. "A complete disaster."

His lower lip began to tremble, and he dropped his face into his hands. For a minute, his body shook with sobs. And then he raised his head and took a deep breath.

"Forgive me barging in on you like this. But I am at my wit's end. I have nowhere else to turn. I have put the entire British Empire at risk."

"Calm yourself, sir," said Holmes. "The Empire has been threatened many times before, and she still stands. Get a hold of yourself, man, and state your case. You can do it."

"The plans for the Observatory," he said.

"Yes, what about them?" asked Holmes. "Have you discovered how he got hold of them?"

"No. But what we did discover was a disaster."

"Explain, please, sir."

"We did a complete inventory of the vault. My worst fears came true. They were not the only plans that were missing."

"What else?" asked Holmes.

"Over one hundred sets of plans are gone. At least sixty are of British warships — almost all of our ships for the past five years. And many of our largest merchant ships, and even several of the newest ferries. All gone. If our enemies or even our allies get hold of them, the advantage of the British Fleet will disappear almost overnight. The design and the capacities of every one of those ships will be known and used against us. It is a disaster, Mr. Holmes. And it happened on my watch."

"Excellent," said Holmes. "I much prefer it when clients come to me on their own behalf rather than sending a surrogate. So, since it is you who are seeking my help, and you are here now, it is best that we get to work. Would you agree, Watson?"

"Indubitably."

"Excellent. Very well, Mr. Phelps, buck up. Time is of the essence. No time for whining. First, I need data, which you will supply with precision and concision to the best of your ability. Then I shall pay a visit to the scene of the crime and conduct an inspection. That is the best way to proceed. Would you agree, Watson?"

"Most certainly."

"Brilliant. Come now, Tadpole Phelps. Play up, play up, and play the game. Let us get to work."

Poor Percy looked at the two of us with bewilderment written all over his face. Had he not been in such a blue funk, I might have laughed. But the spirit that endured being beaten with cricket wickets when he was a lad asserted itself, and he sat up, ready to do his duty.

"Right," said Holmes. "Now who had access to this vault?"

"There was myself, of course; my director, Sir Ughtred; my secretary, Charles; the Tangey family, that is the commissaire, and his wife and daughter who did the charring; three fellows from the engineering department, and two from the Prime Minister's office."

Holmes was writing down all of these.

"Good work. You are sure that is the entire list? No one else?"

"What about those French fellows who have been around for the past few months?" I asked.

"Good heavens, no. We would have to be mad before we would allow foreigners, especially Frenchies, anywhere near our secret documents."

"Quite so," agreed Holmes. "Although it would have been even more unthinkable had they been Italians."

"Oh, yes. I suppose you have a point there."

"Now then, what about those fellows from the Prime minister's office? Were they Admiralty men?"

"No," answered Percy. "They are political appointees. They showed up only after the recent election."

"You mean they are Liberals?" asked Holmes.

"Well, yes, of course. Otherwise, they would not have been appointed."

"Precisely," said Holmes, "and for that reason they should remain on the list of suspects. The Tangey family — I recall that he had a tendency to fall asleep on his duty and that she drinks more than she should."

"They have given exemplary service to me for ten years now. They are rabidly loyal to the Queen, and since coming over to the Admiralty, they have been excellent employees."

"And what about the daughter," asked Holmes. "She must be an independent young woman in her own rights now, is she not?"

"Yes, she is twenty-three years old and a very pretty young lady," said Percy.

"And her character?"

"Nothing out of the ordinary for a girl her age and looks. From time to time a chap might be waiting on the pavement for her after her shift is over, and she sometimes arrives late to work in the mornings. The French fellows flirt with her, but she does her work diligently."

Holmes paused here momentarily. "It might be good to have Forbes put one of the Yard's women on her and see if she has been keeping bad company. What about the others?"

"We haven't seen the engineers for several weeks. They only come when they are delivering an additional set of plans for a new ship. They could not possibly have removed a hundred sets of plans in only two or three visits. They would have to walk past all of the secretaries and typists in broad daylight with a cartload of large schematic drawings."

"But could they have come at night?" asked Holmes.

"Sir, they're union men."

"Right, so they never work into the evening," said Holmes.

"Never, sir."

"Who else is on the list?"

"Only one left is my secretary, Charles Gorot."

"Ah, yes. I remember meeting him. Is he trustworthy?"

Here I had to speak up.

"Holmes," I said. "Mr. Gorot is a Huguenot. His people are quite loyal to the Crown even if their heritage is French."

"Ah, yes, of course," said Holmes. "Those Huguenot people are the sort who think a riotous time is to be had by adding an extra sugar to their tea after mid-week Bible study."

"Exactly," I agreed. During the reception at the Langham, I had had a few minutes to chat directly with Mr. Gorot and was impressed, as I had been seven years ago, with his irreproachable moral rectitude.

"Quite so," said Holmes. "Then we should depart and pay a visit to the Admiralty. Do either of you have obligations on the home front? Wives expecting you for dinner?"

"I am free," said Percy. "Annie came into town for supper with me, but knowing that I would be delayed, I told Charles to go and meet her and keep her from becoming too impatient until I was able to join them."

I, on the other hand, was not free. I had promised Mary that I would be home by six o'clock and it was already just past that hour. I begged off and promised to be available to assist Holmes if he sent for me over the weekend.

We parted. Holmes and Percy took a cab south on Baker Street toward Whitehall. I pressed Shank's pony into service and hurried back to my home by Little Venice, all the while wondering what Holmes would discover in a fortified vault room in the Admiralty.

Chapter Three
The Protective Confession

I remained around my house throughout the weekend, half hoping that I would receive a summons from Holmes, but naught appeared. The newspapers continued to report on the incident at Greenwich, but they had not been informed of the finding of the plans of the interior of the Observatory in Martain Bourdin's pocket, and thus there were no sensational speculations. Once the papers had run out of things to say about the hapless bomber, they began offering stories about incompetent French spies. In the local pub, the talk had moved quickly from fear of bomb tossers to laughter and ridicule at the ineptitude of Frenchmen who blew their own guts away. Soon there was a score of jokes that all began with the line, "Did you hear about the Frenchie who ..."

I was aware that what was taking place was no laughing matter and needed some resolve to focus my concentration on my patients on the following Monday. But shortly after, when I returned to my home and had enjoyed a pleasant dinner with Mary, a note arrived for me. It read:

```
Lestrade coming by at 7. Claims to have
broken the case. If available, please
come to record. S.H.
```

I quickly downed my last cup of tea and hurried on over to 221B Baker Street. A police carriage arrived at the same time as I did and Inspectors Lestrade and Forbes both emerged from it. Together we climbed up to meet Holmes.

Lestrade, utterly smug, was looking like the cat that swallowed the canary.

"Well now, Mr. Sherlock Holmes," he said when we had been seated. "Whilst you were doing all your scientific deducing and hypothesizing and theorizing, we working policemen were doing dogged, basic investigating and it paid off."

"Splendid," said Holmes. "And pray tell me what you did, and what you found."

"We did all those things that a hard-working policeman has to do. We just went out and checked out everything we could about everybody who could possibly have been stealing documents from the Admiralty. It was our checking their bank accounts that broke the case for us."

"Really, and what did you find?"

"There is no end of things you can find, Holmes, when you just do solid looking."

Lestrade was obviously enjoying his moment of triumph and eager to draw it out as long as possible. Holmes smiled at him patiently and played along.

"You don't say," said Holmes. "Please, tell me more. I am all attention."

"Our first suspicion was on those Frenchies. And their bank accounts told us more than we would ever have guessed. Do you know how much those cheese-eaters get from the Quay d'Orsay every month?"

"No. I have no idea."

"Two hundred and twenty-five pounds a month. Every month! That's more than a senior police inspector is paid in six months. It's outrageous, if you ask me."

"Terribly so," said Holmes.

"Ha, but we knew right away that whilst that may be enough to live well in London, it was not enough to be used to pay someone to sell them the plans. You would agree with that, right, Holmes?"

"Perhaps. Pray continue."

"Well we just kept looking, and it surprised us, as I am sure it will you when we found someone who had been making large deposits every week over and above his billet payment. Would you like to guess who it might be, Holmes?"

"You have me on that one, so best you just tell me."

"Charles Gorot," said Lestrade.

I was stunned, and even Holmes was temporarily speechless.

"That is a surprise," said Holmes. "But was there anything to prove that the funds were coming from treasonous acts? He may have a perfectly justifiable reason for them."

"I would say that there was something quite conclusive. I would say that it would even be considered conclusive by Sherlock Holmes. Would you care to guess what it was?"

"I confess, Inspector, that I am at a loss."

"How about ... his confession?"

That was also unexpected. Holmes and I both were stunned. Mr. Gorot, the handsome but austere Huguenot, was the last person we would ever have suspected of such perfidy.

"His bank account said it all," said Lestrade. "I believe it is Mr. Sherlock Holmes who has claimed that a man may lie to the police, to a judge, to his lawyer, to his wife, and even to himself, but he cannot lie to his bank book."

"I do recall saying that," said Holmes.

"His bank records showed that beginning about three months ago he began to make some extra deposits. Every Monday, there they were. First, they started small but then they grew and grew. For the past month, he's been putting in over five hundred pounds every week. Five hundred! Well on his way to becoming a rich young man; a rich young traitor is what he was becoming."

"And pray tell, Inspector, could you explain just how you secured his confession?"

"Weren't difficult at all. Now, I admit, I had right away

suspected those two Frenchies, and never gave a thought to the secretary; him being such a devout Nonconformist believer and all. But we did a routine check of everyone's bank records and saw his deposits. So, when his turn came up for an interview with Inspector Forbes here, he just asked him right out to explain where the money came from. And didn't young Mr. Gorot turn white as a ghost. That's right, isn't it, Forbes?"

"White as a ghost, yes sir, that's what he did. Whiter, if you ask me. And then he says, 'Please excuse me for a moment,' and up he gets and walks away from us. We were sitting in a room in the Admiralty, and he goes back into his office, he does. And we're waiting for him, and he doesn't come back out, which is highly irregular, it is. So, we follows him to his office, and there he is behind his desk, pacing back and forth. He hears us and turns to us, standing up straight and tall, and says, clear as a bell, "I wish to make a full confession of my crime in stealing the plans from the Admiralty vault and selling them.' That's what he said and that's how it happened, Mr. Holmes. So that part of the case is closed, and closed it was by regular hard-working investigating by police officers, it was. Just like Inspector Lestrade says."

"Might you be so kind," said Holmes, "as to inform me as to any reasons he gave?"

"For the benefit of the Republic of France. He's French. That's what he said. His personal profit, too, you can bet."

"If you are saying that two hundred years ago, his people emigrated from France under duress and came to England, then I am aware of that."

"I am only telling you what he told me, Holmes. He has his Frenchness in his blood. He said that deep in his soul, in his spirit, he knew that he was compelled to assist *La République*. So, when the opportunity came along to help himself as well as his native country — his words, not mine, mind you — he had no choice but to serve. That's what he said, isn't it, Inspector Forbes."

"Indeed, it is."

The two inspectors were both looking as proud as peacocks as they delivered this news.

"And to whom," asked Holmes, "did he sell the plans?"

"We do not know that yet," said Lestrade, "but we will soon. He says that he met with a foreign agent over in Southwark. They would meet once a week in a big basement, one that had a ramp down to it, and where cabbies stored their cabs when they weren't using them. It was dark down there, and he said the fellow stood behind a pillar and would not let his face be seen and he talked in a disguised voice, as if he were speaking from deep back in his throat. And Gorot claims he has no idea as to his identity, but he had a French accent and said he was an agent of the president. Whoever he is, we'll find him. I have men out now, and we are rounding up all our informers in Southwark. It won't be long until we find the fellow. And once again, Mr. Holmes, we'll find him using dogged police work and wearing out our shoe leather."

"My congratulations," said Holmes, "on solving the case so far, and my best wishes for success on the remainder."

"Thank you, Mr. Holmes," said Inspector Forbes, and Lestrade grunted something to the same effect.

Once the two inspectors had departed from the room, I turned to Holmes.

"Must say, Holmes. I did not see that one coming. I would have guessed the Frenchies as well, or maybe the Liberals from Westminster, but never Charles."

"Nor would I," said Holmes. "Nor would I."

He then went silent and closed his eyes, but as I watched him, I could see that he was moving his head slowly from side to side, then dropping it a fraction and moving it sideways yet again. He kept this up for several minutes as if tracing a grid in his mind. When he opened his eyes, they were bright and unblinking. He turned slowly to me.

"I fear the police will become rather frustrated looking for their basement. There is not a single basement used for cabs and carriages in all of Southwark."

"Why then, would Gorot make it up?" I asked. "That makes no sense at all. His confession will send him off to prison for at least ten years. Adding lies to it will not look good in front of a judge. Why not tell the whole truth?"

"He must," said Holmes, "be protecting someone."

"But who?"

"That, my dear doctor, is what I intend to discover."

For the next three days, I heard nothing from Holmes. The incident at Greenwich had now vanished from the pages of the press and had been replaced by the news that a couple of ambitious chaps, Simon Marks and Thomas Spencer, announced the opening in Manchester of a "modern" store selling a multitude of different goods. The press experts in business and commerce predicted that it would be a flash-in-the-pan and fail.

On the Thursday of that week, I came back to my home after a day of seeing patients in the hospital and my medical office and enjoyed a lovely dinner hour with my wife. After dinner had been finished and cleared away, we chatted briefly about the reception last week, the Hottentotten problem in the southwest Cape, and the latest news from America. We had gone on nicely for about ten minutes when she abruptly changed the subject.

"Darling," she said, "I need to ask you to do me a favor."

"Anything, my precious. What can I do for the love of my life?"

"It's about Annie."

"What about Annie? You saw her today for lunch, did you not?"

"I did, darling, and I am hoping that you could do something to help her."

"What can I do to help?"

"Could you," she asked, "arrange a meeting between her and Sherlock Holmes?"

"Most certainly. Shall I try to arrange it for Saturday, so that Percy does not have to miss time from the Admiralty? He is frightfully busy with this French treaty matter."

Mary smiled at me for a moment. "No, darling. It is to be between Annie and Sherlock only. Percy cannot know about it."

I was staggered by what she said.

"Mary, dearest. Are you asking me to aid and abet a woman to deceive her husband? To do something behind his back and deliberately withhold it from him? Why ... why that is unthinkable."

I was aghast.

"John, darling, it is all for Percy's good. It will all come to light when you hear what she has to say to Sherlock. Annie would prefer that you and I be present to bear witness. Please, John, do trust me on this matter. All I can tell you is that what she is doing is awfully brave and Sherlock Holmes is the only one she can turn to."

I was not at all at ease about this, but I had learned over the years, as most husbands do, that a wife's solemn requests are a thing to heed, so I sent a note off to Holmes requesting a meeting at his earliest convenience. He replied immediately saying that he would be free tomorrow afternoon, and would be more than happy to meet with the three of us.

Chapter Four
Down a Slippery Slope

Mary and I took a cab over to Baker Street the following afternoon and had the driver wait until Mrs. Phelps arrived from Waterloo Station. When she did, she departed her cab and entered ours so that the three of us could have a few minutes together before entering 221B. I confess that I was somewhat surprised by her appearance. Just the previous week, I had chatted with her at the reception at the Langham, and she was resplendent in a gown and jewelry. Today, she looked for all the world like the daughter of a Northumberland merchant and quite prepared to do serious business. She was plain in both face and dress and her countenance, which had shone so brightly last week, was markedly pale.

Neither she nor Mary disclosed anything about what she was going to say to Holmes. All we did was to assure her that this formidable man, who she had met seven years earlier and obediently followed his instructions, was not terrifying, but could be a congenial gentleman and usually was.

Holmes welcomed us warmly into the front room of 221B and, although I knew it pained him to do so, chatted briefly about the weather and the great horse manure debate, the latest outrage in the press after some professor had proven that at the present rate and growth of production, in fifty years every street in London would be buried under nine feet of manure. We all forced ourselves to chuckle at the prospect before Holmes turned to Mrs. Phelps and took command of the interview.

"My dear lady," he began, "seven years ago you were the lovely young fiancée of Percy Phelps, nursing him through that terrible time of crisis. He would never be where he is today had it not been for your loving care. And we would never have discovered the stolen naval treaty had it not been for your very astute following of my instructions. You have my admiration and respect on both counts."

Tactfully, Holmes made no mention of her naivete in not suspecting that it was her brother, Joseph, who had so betrayed his sister and his future brother-in-law. He had fled, most likely to America, and had been heard from no more.

"No doubt," Holmes went on, "you are here concerning the current issue of the thefts that have taken place at the Admiralty."

"Yes, sir, that is why I am here."

"And no doubt, it also relates directly to the news you heard from your husband that his trusted secretary, Charles Gorot, was the culprit."

"Yes, sir, that is correct."

"And you are privy to some highly sensitive information that proves his innocence. Is that correct?"

Annie Phelps face took on that same look of wonder that I had seen on so many faces of young women who had come to seek the help of Sherlock Holmes and were stunned by his foreknowledge and insight into their situations.

"Why, yes sir it is. How did you know that?"

I gave a bit of a cough and glared at Holmes. He was making the poor young woman feel even more ill at ease than she obviously already was. He read the rebuke on my face.

"Really, Mrs. Phelps, it is nothing if not inevitable. The only recent development in this case has been Mr. Gorot's confession — his so-called confession as far as I am concerned — and that must be what brought you here. That you are in possession of some highly sensitive information is proclaimed by your keeping this meeting secret from your husband. And I have never believed for one minute that Charles Gorot's confession and explanation made any sense."

"Why not?" I interrupted and asked.

"Good heavens, Watson, the man may be intensely

religious to the point of believing in the literal truth of talking snakes and Balaam's ass, floating axe heads, and the temporary halting of the Copernican solar system, but that does not mean that he has so far dismissed his faculties of reason as to believe for one minute that it is worth spending a minute of your life in prison for such an idiotic cause and helping France recover its long-lost glory. The man may be a devout zealot, but he is not *that* stupid. And his story about the basement in Southwark was a clear fabrication. So, please, Mrs. Phelps, continue. Kindly tell me how you came to hold this knowledge. Would I be correct in assuming that it came directly to you from Mr. Gorot, or perhaps indirectly? Which was it?"

Now that the issue was revealed, Annie Phelps visibly relaxed.

"Directly, sir."

"And how did that come about?" asked Holmes.

"We shared many dinners and private conversations together."

Goodness gracious, I thought to myself. That was a very strange thing for a married woman to admit, and she seemed not in the least embarrassed by it.

"Please, let me explain," she said.

"I wish you would," said Holmes. "I am quite intrigued."

"Percy and I were married not long after the terrible incident with the naval treaty. Our home, as you know, is in Woking, and it has not been practical for him to return every night and then go back into London every morning. He stays overnight at his club from Monday through Thursday. But he is a most attentive husband and sets aside time every Friday beginning in the late afternoon for the two of us to be together. I would come to London, he would depart his office by half-past four, and the two of us would take in the sites, walk in the parks, have a lovely supper together, and occasionally go to a play in the West End. And then we would stay at one of the select hotels. These were very special times for us, and we valued them highly."

"That all sounds quite lovely," said Holmes. "But how does Charles Gorot come into the picture?"

"As Percy advanced in his career, especially after his appointment to such a responsible position at the Admiralty, there were many times, to his great frustration, that he could not leave his desk at four-thirty. Sometimes he would be delayed for half an hour, but often it would be for two or even three hours. He is a most considerate gentleman as well as a loving husband, and he was deeply distressed to think that I would be awkwardly sitting in a café or a posh restaurant waiting for him. Thus, if he knew he was going to be quite delayed, he would send Charles, his secretary, over to meet me, with the instruction that he should amuse me and carry on a conversation with me until Percy was free of the office. Then he would meet us and thank Charles, and Charles would depart.

"At first, my conversations with Charles were stilted and difficult. We would chat about the weather, about the décor of the restaurant, or about stories in the news. However, in the past five years, I have met with Charles over one hundred times, and many of those times we had to wait two or three hours for Percy to arrive. We became more and more familiar with each other, as did our conversations. Eventually, we abandoned all those walls that people erect around themselves, and we talked to each other ... from our hearts. Our conversations became more and more intimate, and we shared, you might say, the secrets of our souls."

"And did you," Holmes asked, "also fall in love with him?"

Again, I was annoyed by Holmes's utter lack of discretion and tact and was about to interrupt, but I felt a sharp kick to my ankle from Mary, whose look instructed me to keep quiet.

Annie Phelps was blushing, but her reply was not what I had expected.

"If you are asking me, Mr. Holmes, if I came to care very deeply for Charles, to be terribly fond of him, then yes. I did. And he developed similar feelings for me. Did our friendship ever transgress and enter into any forbidden realm? No. We were both completely circumspect. We never engaged in any physical contact beyond his taking my hand for a brief moment when we met, in the manner of a perfect gentleman."

"Yes," said Holmes. "But apparently something did take place. Otherwise I rather doubt that you would be here."

"What happened was much worse."

"Was it? Pray, go on."

"Charles, as you know comes from a very devout Huguenot family. They are very severe in their refusal to partake of the things of this world as they call them. They would never touch a drop of alcohol; they do not allow tobacco; dancing is forbidden as is the theater; a music hall is the devil's playground; and the sin of gambling is a sure pathway to hell and eternal damnation."

"I am aware," said Holmes, "of the ascetic convictions of some of the Reformist sects."

"I fear that I led Charles down the broad path and through the wide gate that leads to destruction. It was not my intent, I assure you. But whereas Charles had been raised believing that even a sip of an intoxicating drink is a deadly sin, I grew up next door to Scotland. My father was convinced that the Scots were barely evolved beyond barbarians, but he did credit them with discovering the 'water of life' as he called it, or Scottish whiskey. He acquired a great fondness for it, and so did my mother, and so did my brother … and so did I.

"When Charles and I would sit and chat for hours, he would order endless cups of tea, and I would ask for a fine single malt mixed with water. If Percy were quite late in arriving, I might have enjoyed several glasses of Scotch before he showed up."

"Pardon me, Mrs. Phelps," said Holmes. "Are you saying that you were prepared to be somewhat inebriated when meeting your husband?" Holmes sounded as if he were honestly shocked by such behavior. Mary laughed.

"Oh, Sherlock," she said. "Sherlock, you are *such a bachelor.*"

He gave her a rather harsh but puzzled look. She laughed again.

"Please, Annie. Enlighten him," said Mary.

Mrs. Phelps could not resist a sly smile. "It is not without reason that since the dawn of time, men have offered copious amounts of wine and spirits to women. By the time Percy arrived I would be feeling, shall we say, more than a little amorous. I would insist that we abandon the plans for a walk, or even the theater, and proceed directly to the hotel and order room service. My husband was never angry with me. Need I say more Mr. Holmes?"

Now Holmes was blushing.

"No. Please do not. Kindly return to your conversations with Mr. Gorot."

"Very well, then. I would tease him about his tea and, in jest, kept encouraging him to try 'just a wee dram' of Scotch. Well, he did try, and that was the beginning of the slippery slope. He acquired a taste for it as well and soon would match me glass for glass and then some. But, I am afraid, that was not the end of it. My dear Northumbrian family used to love to pass a Saturday night playing every known game of cards. As Charles and I had endless hours to pass, beginning a year ago, I taught him how to play bridge and whist. Now Charles has an absolutely brilliant mind and he not only learned quickly, he soon was trouncing me in almost every round.

"Recently, he made a confession to me and swore me to secrecy concerning it. Had he not been put in jail and charged with treason, I would never have broken that promise."

"I am waiting," said Holmes, "rather impatiently, for you to break it. I assume that is the reason for our meeting. Please, get to the point, Mrs. Phelps."

"Charles admitted that several months back, for the first time in his life, he joined a club in which card-playing and other forms of gambling took place. He tried just a few hands of whist and came away with twenty pounds in his pocket. He started to visit the clubs every weekend, and he began to play for higher and higher stakes. He is so clever; he has such an exceptional mind for numbers, and an unfailing memory, that he won more and more money. He was soon winning several hundred pounds every week. Every Monday he would deposit his winnings into his bank account."

"Ah, ha," said Holmes. "So that is the source of the bank deposits that Lestrade discovered. But that is hardly reason to make a false confession for treason. What else is there to the story, Mrs. Phelps?"

She lowered her eyes and spoke in a hushed voice.

"Charles confessed to me that he had engaged in some activities that were depraved. As you must be aware, sir, the gambling clubs attract some rather loose women and there he was, a handsome young man, with a brilliant mind, a respected billet with the Admiralty, and now rather rich. Women were throwing themselves at his feet, and he succumbed. Of late, he has acquired a mistress. He says that she is beautiful and brilliant and he has fallen hopelessly in love with her. He seems quite besotted and ready to die for her."

"Madam," said Holmes. "He is not the first gentleman to acquire a mistress, I assure you. And I also assure you that I have never heard of any other man sending himself off to prison for a decade after doing so. You are making no sense at all."

"Oh, don't you see, Mr. Holmes? It is about his family. I knew it must be from our many intimate conversations. His father died when he was only sixteen years old. His mother and his younger brothers and sisters all look up to him as if he is a saint. He is admired and respected highly by all the members of his church. If it became known that he was living a double life and that he had become utterly dissolute, his family would be shamed. He fears his mother would die of pain and unspeakable disappointment. He is terrified that the truth will out. I know these things because I visited him in his prison cell on Sunday. I confronted him. I looked into his eyes. I could see into his soul. I told him that I had discerned the reasons for his confession and knew that he had given a false statement to protect his family. I know his spirit, sir, and I persisted. At first, he denied it, but then he thought it over carefully and he came clean and admitted it all to me."

"Did he now?" said Holmes. "So, he prefers to be branded a traitor and sent to jail? How can that possibly be less a shameful thing than debauchery?"

"But, sir. Do you not see? After he admitted to me that he had made a false confession, he said that his family would be devastated if they knew he had given his life over to the pleasures of the flesh, but they would believe that he acted treasonously if he did it *for the French*. His people are Huguenots. They are *French*. They would understand. They would shake their heads at his foolishness, but they would begrudgingly admire him. That's why he is doing this."

A cold hard look came over Holmes's face. "You have informed me, Mrs. Phelps, that a highly respected young man, with a wonderful future in front of him, is no more than a degenerate hypocrite. He gave a false statement to the police to prevent the exposure of his debauchery which, after meeting with you, he now recants. You admit to loving him, and you are now asking me to intervene and rescue him from the wages of his sins. Pray tell, why, in the name of all that is holy, should I lift a finger to help him?"

Mrs. Phelps returned his look with a hard one of her own, and I witnessed a flash of the steely resolve that I had seen seven years ago in Woking.

"Because Scotland Yard believes him. And Mr. Sherlock Holmes now knows the truth, and if you do nothing, then Sherlock Holmes will be allowing the real criminal to walk away scot free. Is that what you wish to do Mr. Holmes?"

She had discerned the chink in his armor and stabbed through it. Holmes was visibly angry. He hated being pushed around, or manipulated, especially by a woman. His hands gripped the arms of the chair he was sitting in, and his knuckles whitened. I had watched him feign anger at clients in the past, but he was not pretending. He was furious.

But he had no choice.

He stood up, strode over to the door and opened it. Gesturing to Mrs. Phelps to leave.

"Good day, madam. I will pay a visit to Mr. Gorot on Monday. By the end of next week, I assure you that he will be released. I trust you will have a pleasant evening ... with your husband."

Annie Phelps looked as if she were about to return the jibe, but she restrained herself, nodded, rose and departed. We followed her out of the room, down the stairs, and out on to Baker Street.

"I have the impression," she said to Mary and me, "that he does not like me."

"Can you blame him?" said I.

"But what could I do?"

"You did," said Mary, "what you had to do and it is done. In a few days, Sherlock will get over his anger and will have a grudging respect for you. It has happened before when he has been bested by a woman."

"Oh, I hope you're right," said Annie. Then she pulled out her watch. "I have to meet Percy in an hour. Is there any place where around here where a girl can find a decent glass of Scotch? I could truly use one."

Chapter Five
Huguenots and Anarchists

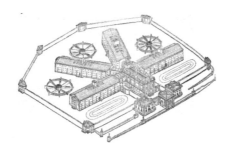

 note from Holmes came to my medical office at noon on Monday. It ran:

```
Meeting Charles Gorot at Wandsworth at 4.
Please join me. Meet at front gate.
Holmes.
```

I rushed through my afternoon patients and caught a cab south through the park and across the Battersea Bridge into Wandsworth. Holmes was pacing back and forth on the pavement in front of the main gate of Wandsworth Prison.

The prison was a somewhat new facility. It had been built

according to the most humane principles of the mid-century and each prisoner had his own cell and toilet. The six radiating spokes and the spacious grounds removed the accusation of horrendous treatment of criminals that had been leveled at Newgate at other London prisons.

Charles Gorot was housed in the north wing, where those men were kept whose crime had not involved physical violence. Prison officials led us to his cell and opened the door. He appeared to be surprised to see us.

"Why hello there," he said, quite pleasantly. "To what do I owe the honor of a visit from Sherlock Holmes and Dr. Watson? I do hate to disappoint you, but there's not much of a story here for readers of the Strand."

"Our visit," snapped Holmes, "has nothing to do with the Strand. We are here because the true traitor is free on the streets of London, while you are in prison because of lying in your confession in order to save your mum's precious feelings. And this nonsense has to end."

His face displayed shock. "Annie spoke to you, did she not? I made her promise not to say anything to anybody. Dear God, now what am I going to do?"

He sat back down on the edge of his bed and buried his face in his hands.

"What you are going to do, Mr. Gorot," said Holmes, "is admit your sinful actions to your mother, and then to the police, and recant from your false confession. And you must do it immediately. Enough is enough."

"I'm sorry, Mr. Holmes. I simply cannot do that. It would break my mother's heart. I would rather spend the rest of my life in jail."

"I am not giving you a choice, Mr. Gorot. I have made arrangements for your mother to visit you here tomorrow. Either you will tell her the truth and tell the same to the police, or I will."

"Have you," said Gorot, "no feelings at all for a dear devout woman? Can you not understand that she would rather die than know how I have failed her?" He touched his hand, quite dramatically, to his chest as he spoke.

"She will not," replied Holmes, "be the first mother in England to be deeply disappointed in her eldest son. From Queen Victoria, with her dissolute son, our Prince of Wales, right down to the humblest scullery maid, mothers have had their hearts broken by their sons. You mother will survive and will have to live with the shame and so will you. You have until tomorrow at this time. Good day, sir."

Holmes turned and abruptly left the cell. I followed.

The following day was warm and sunny, and after supper, my wife and I enjoyed a cup of tea by the open window of our front room. I brought her up-to-date on what all had transpired in the Admiralty case, and she kept me informed about her work with the various social reform movements to which she devoted her time and energy.

Whilst we were enjoying a cup of tea, a cab pulled up to the curb and its passenger, a woman alone, descended to the pavement in front of us. She was a lady well into her fifties,

51

but was tall and slender and carried herself upright, in an almost military posture. She was dressed in a conservative gray dress and a light black jacket. Her graying hair appeared to have been gathered up and arranged under her simple black felt hat. Her shoes would be described, speaking charitably, as sensible, and she was entirely unadorned with any trace of jewelry or cosmetics. Her face immediately gave away her identity, and I rose from my chair to open our door to Mrs. Gorot.

"I apologize for interrupting you," she said. "I wish to speak to Dr. Watson."

"I am he," I said and gave a respectful nod. "Please, come in. This is my wife, Mary and no apology is necessary. May we offer you a cup of tea? I suspect that there might be one or two things you are interested in chatting about. You are Mrs. Gorot, Charles's mother, if I am not mistaken."

She smiled and took a seat with us. "Thank you. Yes. I am Mrs. Othniel Gorot, and yes, I am here because of my son."

Mary had quickly put out another cup and saucer and poured a cup for our guest. The lady took a sip before speaking again.

"I had called first at Baker Street. Mr. Holmes was not in, but his landlady was kind enough to give me your address. I am sorry for barging in upon you without warning, but I felt it important to do so."

"Mrs. Gorot," I said, "considering what you must have been through during the past few days, no excuse is necessary. Mothers have every right to do whatever they feel necessary in matters concerning their sons."

"Thank you, doctor. You are most gracious. My reason for stopping by is to thank you and Mr. Sherlock Holmes for knocking some sense into the thick skull of my oldest son. The good Lord gave him a brilliant mind, but I could not believe that he had been so idiotically stupid."

"Madam?"

"Honestly, doctor, can you imagine anything more unbelievable than a young man sending himself off to prison for a decade as a way of trying to hide sowing his wild oats?"

I was surprised, although I later thought that I should not have been. Everything about this woman said *sensible* in upper case.

"That is an interesting observation," I said.

"Interesting? Perhaps it is, but it is also true. Our Lord divinely told us that he had not come to call the righteous but sinners to repentance. Had Charles not strayed from the straight and narrow and indulged his youthful animal spirits, he would not have been a normal young man. I repeated the words of the Lord to the woman taken in adultery. I told him, 'Neither do I condemn thee. Go and sin no more' Like any sinner, my son has to confess his sins before the Lord, and give up his sinful ways, and his mistress, which may be the most difficult for him. Then he must trust in the Lord to direct his paths from now on. That is my prayer for him, and I will keep praying that prayer every day"

"Ah, a very good idea," I said. "You were, it appears, not as surprised and shocked by your son's recent past as he claimed to us that you might be."

She took another sip of her tea and continued.

"I also reminded him that he is his father's son. Some things are in the blood and we might as well all face up to them."

"Madam?"

"His father, Mr. Othniel Gorot, who passed away and went on to glory some twelve years ago, spent an entire decade doing the same and much worse. After completing his schooling, he took the Queen's shilling and joined the BEF. For seven years ran around the world shooting defenseless natives in the name of the Empire; legalized murder as far as our church is concerned. After completing his term in the forces, he gallivanted around the Continent, mostly in Italy, drinking and carousing and devoting his passions to one silly cause after another. For at least three years he even descended to the depths of depravity and became a *socialist*."

This final word was uttered in a hushed tone, lest anyone passing by might be listening in.

"His terrible life might have continued in that direction had he not paid a visit back to his family—a fine, upright family from our church who had been faithfully praying for him every day—and agreed, under duress, to attend a Sunday evening church service. There he came under the sound of the gospel, was convicted of his sins by the Holy Spirit, and gave his heart to the Lord. Like the Apostle on the road to Damascus, he immediately turned from darkness toward the light and lived a highly respectable life until the day he died. He worked diligently as a tailor, as is common among we Protestants of French heritage. He established his own business, and we were blessed with prosperity, so much so that enough money had been set aside for me to help Charles and his younger brothers and sisters acquire an excellent education."

"Did Charles," my wife asked our guest, "not know about his father's past?"

The lady took another sip of tea before responding. "In the year before Othniel passed away, he and Charles had many father and son talks together. I had always thought that my husband was imparting the lessons he had learned from his past life to his son, but Charles claims that it was all news to him and he acted terribly shocked and disappointed. He was, however, relieved greatly at the same time and agreed that he would immediately contact the police and recant his false confession. I fully expect that he will do so tomorrow morning, and that he will be released shortly after."

We chatted on for a few more minutes and then Mrs. Gorot stood up and again thanked me for whatever role I had played in helping her son. I assured her that I would pass on her sentiments to Holmes, whose role far surpassed mine.

As she departed I thought that it was odd that a son could be so far wrong in perceiving his mother's need for protection that he would be willing to spend a decade in prison quite unnecessarily. But he was still young, and his ability to reason would remain weakened by his hormones for several years to come.

"So, John, my dear," said my wife after Mrs. Gorot had departed in her cab, "what happens now?"

"I suppose that Holmes and the Yard will have to go back to investigating all the other possible suspects on the list."

"And you, my dear, will be ready to help him."

"Perhaps, if he calls me. You never know."

"Oh, darling, you know he is going to call for you, and you will rush to his side. There is nothing that my wonderful husband enjoys more."

He did not call for me for the rest of the week, but on Friday afternoon a note arrived. It ran:

```
Would you be so kind as to drop in on me
for a few minutes tomorrow morning? Do
offer my excuses to your dear wife for
pulling you away from home on a Saturday.
Holmes.
```

I offered my apologies as well as Holmes's to Mary. She merely laughed merrily.

"Darling, I married you for better or for worse, but not for lunch. Go and enjoy your adventure with Sherlock. Just try to be back home for supper, and do not forget to duck before you get shot."

The following morning, I was up and out of the house before eight o'clock, arriving at 221B Baker Street soon after.

Holmes took one look at me as I entered the familiar room.

"We will have to work on your appearance," he said.

"What in heaven's name for?" I said. I had taken some pains to look relaxed and informal but nevertheless rather smart.

"You would look appropriate were we about to go for a stroll along Regent Street," said Holmes. "However, we are going to the monthly meeting of all the assorted anarchists in London. You will have to look disheveled, acceptably unfashionable, and impossible for anyone to recognize. Wait here."

He departed briefly into the bedroom and returned bearing an armful of clothes and shoes and a small cloth sack.

"Here, pull these on," he said. "In the sack is a wig, a paste-on mustache, some spirit glue, and wig powder to lighten your hair. Please get to work whilst I do the same."

"Would you mind, Holmes," I asked, "taking a moment to tell me what we are up to?"

"As might be expected, Lestrade was not at all happy when Master Gorot withdrew his false confession. Scotland Yard now has to get back to their hard-working police work and look into the affairs of every possible suspect on their list. He remains convinced, and I am inclined to agree with him, that the fellow who blew himself up may have conveniently pointed us to a larger plot by the international fraternity of anarchists who now live in London. Thus, I am to infiltrate the Club Autonomie, the gathering place for the entire lot of them."

"And they meet there, openly?" said I. "On a regular basis? How can that be?"

"Oh, it is really quite clever of the Yard. If they were to close down the club, all they would do would be to disburse the members, force them into secret cells and clandestine meetings, and not be able to keep track of them at all. By letting them meet, they can watch who is coming and going and, when necessary at times, send spies to infiltrate it. This morning is one of those times, and we are the spies."

"And our identities? Who are we to be? Somehow, I do not think it would be practical to announce ourselves as Sherlock Holmes and Dr. Watson," I said.

Holmes chuckled. "Bravo. No, my dear doctor, you are Mr. Barry O'Rouke, and you are a lowly orderly at St. Bart's. Your family moved to London from County Cork when you were an infant, which explains your lack of an Irish accent. Do you think you can manage that?"

"I'm certain I can, and what about you?"

"I will be an aged, decrepit bookseller."

"Are you not getting a little tired of that role?" I teased.

"It was either that or a clergyman. Somehow I thought the latter might be somewhat suspect at a gathering of the faithful anarchists."

"You could go as an ardent pastor of one of the reformist sects?"

He smiled back at me. "I fear I am profoundly unsuited for such an impersonation. Those good people do not permit the use of tobacco."

At the bottom of the stairs, we encountered Mrs. Hudson. She looked shocked for an instant and then broke into gales of laughter, her entire body shaking. She did not cease laughing at us until she had shooed us out of the door.

It was a short walk across our corner of London to Tottenham Court Road and south to Windmill Street. The club appeared to be no more than a shop front, crammed in amongst other shops along a parade. Other than the name of the club above the door, there was nothing to indicate what it was, but we followed some chaps, who looked much the same as Holmes and me, into the hall beyond the entrance.

"Bonjour, monsieur," said a tall, somewhat stooped, silver-haired fellow. "I have not met you here before. *Bienvenue.*"

"Why, thank you," I replied, and prepared to deliver my well-rehearsed introduction of myself. "It is my first time."

"*Pourquoi*, comrade, are you here?"

"I have worked," I said, hoping not to sound like a gentleman doctor, "as an orderly. Every day I see the rich receiving excellent care whilst the poor cannot pay for even the most basic medical services. I am angry about it, and I am not going to take it any longer."

"*Mais oui*, comrade. And is it not true that all those rich doctors, they think they are God himself, the way they treat the nurses and orderlies? They are too pig-headed to know that it is the working people of the hospital who give the true care to the sick and dying. They are the ones who wash their bodies, who lift and carry them from their beds to the operating tables, who change their bedclothes, who empty their bedpans, who wipe their bottoms, and who comfort them when they are dying. And yet they are paid a pittance of what is paid to a doctor. This is not fair, is it, comrade?"

I was not expecting that line of insights and questions, so I mumbled some form of agreement and changed the topic of the conversation.

"You are French," I said, stating the obvious.

"*Mais oui.* But of course. Many members of Le Club Autonomie are French. London is our city of refuge, as it is for the anarchists from Russia, Spain, Germany, Holland, and Italy. Our lives in our own countries, sadly, would be very short, so we are refugees in England."

"Oh, I did not know that," I said, honestly.

We took our seats and a rugged, red-faced Welshman called the meeting to order. Then, the entire congregation of well over one hundred of us stood and lustily sang the Internationale, first in English and then in French. Although my French is far from fluent, it struck me that the song was far more powerful in that language:

And then they sang it yet again in Russian. But, as I have no knowledge at all of that tongue, I could not sing along.

Once we had worked through all three versions, the room let out a joyous yell, during which several socialist slogans were shouted from some of the more enthusiastic members. Up to this point, the meeting was not much different than a revival meeting held by the Baptists.

The comrade who had called the meeting order returned to the pulpit.

"Let us stand, our heads unbowed, for a moment of silence, as a tribute to another martyr for the cause of the revolution. As you know, our comrade, Brother Martain Bourdin, sacrificed his young life for the workers of the world. Let his dedication be an example to all of us."

"Hear, hear," and other affirmations were heard. My only thought, which I had to stifle, was that blowing your hand off and disemboweling yourself whilst accomplishing nothing was not the most exemplary path to follow. One of the members said something in French, and I glanced across to the far front corner of the room to see who might be expressing the sentiments of La République. I immediately gave an elbow to Holmes.

"Look," I whispered, "at those two in the front corner. The tall, good-looking chaps."

"Yes," he nodded back. "I see them. What of them?"

"They were at the reception at the Langham. They are the French naval captains I told you about."

Holmes straightened his curved body to get a better view and looked at Captains François and August as closely as he could without becoming conspicuous himself. He then turned and mouthed the words, "Thank you, Watson," and slumped back into his decrepit bookseller posture.

The chairman of the meeting continued with various announcements regarding the annual fall picnic at Kew, the efforts being made on behalf of imprisoned comrades in various countries on the Continent, and the decision by the Committee for Administrative Concerns regarding a re-organization of the Quartermaster's functions.

"As you know," the fellow droned on, "our lawful club was raided by the police following the death of Comrade Bourdin. They came here and in violation of British Law, forced their entry and undertook a fruitless search for dynamite. It was agreed by the Committee that a special commendation should be made to Comrade Ivan Gollanz, our Quartermaster, who has diligently enforced the Club's ban on having any illegal substances allowed on our premises."

A round of applause was given for the Quartermaster, after which some chap in near the back shouted out, "Did you say 'allowed' or 'allowed to be found?'" His question elicited a round of laughter and applause for the deviously diligent Quartermaster.

Following several other business items that led me to marvel at the traditional organizational skills of a group of anarchists, the chairman called on the first speaker. Up to the pulpit stepped Captain François l'Olannais.

"*Bonjour, mes comrades,* he began. "It is my honor to deliver a short monograph and by doing so, impart to our friends in London some of the lessons learned from the experience of the Commune in Paris during the eventful year of 1870."

His English was eloquent, even with a French accent.

"The marvelous experience of the Commune, when, for two glorious months, the proletariat truly were dictators and masters of their own destinies, has been praised in song, poetry, paintings, dance, and music. It stands as an example to the world of what citizens can achieve when we work together to throw off the yoke of the ruling class and the bourgeoisie. Tragically, these golden days did not last long. Previous studies have entirely dealt with the military failure of *La Guarde Nationale* to defend the citizens against the army. This morning, I shall endeavor to present an alternative understanding and thus enrich our critical intelligence. There was another factor at play, and it was the age-old issue of money. Thus, my monograph is called *Lessons from the Commune: The Economic Consequences of the Peace.*"

Having introduced his talk, he went carried on, rather brilliantly I thought, to explain the ways and means of paying the expenses of a revolution. It was not only an army that marched on its stomach, it was also the militia, and the local revolutionary committees or what the Russians referred to as a *soviet*. All of the people who were in the front lines of the struggle still had to be fed and clothed. Their children had to have schools, and their elderly and sick had to be cared for.

The elegant captain made a highly persuasive case and concluded by humbly offering the services of himself and his colleague, Captain Duhaut-Cilly, if assistance was needed by any anarchist movement in England in managing their financial affairs. When he concluded, he was greeted with polite although not particularly thunderous applause.

Following him came several other speakers, each of whom spoke briefly. Two of them, one French and the other Greek, were passionate about their particular subjects. The Scottish chap was, as would be expected, highly practical howbeit rather dull.

The crowd was getting a bit restless. We had been sitting attentively for nearly two hours, and I sensed that they had become impatient for the main event that had been promised. The restlessness changed to a mood of anticipation when the chairman bounded up to the pulpit and, smiling broadly, sought silence from the audience.

"Brothers and sisters, comrades all, we have saved the best until the last. Our honored guest is loved, revered, and respected by all of us and by our fellow revolutionaries in Europe and America. She has, from her own pocket, given money to many revolutionary movements throughout Europe and we are very grateful for her generosity. Comrades, our final speaker is not only the one of the most admired of our movement, she is by far the most attractive. Allow me to introduce, without any further delay, our beloved sister and comrade, Mrs. Lucy Goldman."

The crowd leapt to their feet and applauded enthusiastically. I joined with them so as not to appear conspicuous. Through the sea of unkempt heads, I could see a figure standing in the front row and walking up to the platform. As she ascended the steps, her long brunette locks swayed back and forth across her shoulders. When she arrived at the pulpit, she turned and faced the crowd.

I stopped clapping, and my mouth opened involuntarily. Standing in the pulpit, dressed in plain clothing, but still dazzling, was the woman I had been introduced to only a short time ago as Princess Casamassima.

Chapter Six
Dazzling Violence

She smiled a perfect smile and nodded humbly in response to the applause. The adulation eventually subsided, and we resumed our seats.

"Comrades, you are very kind to me" she began in a strong, clear voice and distinctive American accent. "Please, let me assure you that there is only one thing I accomplished that has permitted my ability to help pay for your courageous activities. I married a very rich but rather stupid Italian prince. All I had to do was to be smarter than he was and, I assure you, it was not difficult."

This admission was met with a round of hearty laughter, followed by more applause. Then she continued, her tone both congenial and authoritative.

"Comrades," she continued, "my colleague and eloquent Captain François has explained to you the economic lessons of the Commune. It is not my place to argue with his learned research. But my desire today is to bring what I believe to be the greatest lesson of the Commune. I have given to my talk the title of *Lessons from Communarde Louise Michel: Education and Violence Can Never Be Separated.*"

Here she was interrupted by applause.

"Comrade Louise was a dear member of this Club until she recently returned to her beloved, native France. I have heard from her just last week, and she informs me that she is safe and is already teaching again, while at the same time stirring up the impoverished masses against the cruelties and injustice of government. Over the past several years, it was my honor to sit at her feet and learn from her. I was not worthy to do so, but I had told her my story, and she took me under her wing. Now, allow me to impart my humble story to you, as it will help you to understand the convictions I have embraced in my heart and the conclusions I have reached with respect to the revolutionary actions we must take if we are to have any hope of seeing the dictatorship of the proletariat in our lifetime."

The earnest young woman was as accomplished a public speaker as any man I had ever listened to. She began by telling us how she and her family had lived a peaceful life in the city of Strasbourg. Her father was French and her mother

German, a situation that was common in the towns and villages of Alsace. Her father was a tailor and was reasonably prosperous, but when the war took over the province, he was declared an enemy by the advancing German forces and, though unarmed, was killed by the German troops. His execution took place in front of his wife and young daughter.

Mrs. Lucy went on to tell us how she and her mother had fled to Paris with nothing but the clothes on their back. Her mother was able to earn a few francs as a seamstress, but soon the Prussian army laid siege to the city, and her mother fled again, this time to America. The loss of the husband and father left a great hole in the young woman's soul and, as she grew and learned, she came to understand that the true enemy of the people was not the Prussian army who won the war, nor the French who lost it, nor the English who could have intervened and stopped the senseless slaughter, but who stood back, watched and did nothing.

She then explained, to a warmly appreciative audience, how the difficulties of her early life had fostered her political ideology. The foundation of her faith, as she called it, was her education in the facts and data of social science. Her own studies, combined with the teaching she had received from the esteemed communard Louise Michel, had led her to the truth that anarchy must take place before any just society can be established. Whilst I did not agree with her, I felt genuinely sympathetic to her own pilgrim's progress.

Then she lost me.

"We all know," she admonished, "that you cannot make an omelette without breaking a few eggs," and she justified the assassination of crowned heads and their family members, or even innocent bystanders as a necessary price to pay in order to achieve justice for the masses. She made reference to a series of actions by anarchists — the bombings in Paris at the Opéra and the Chambre des Députés and the killing of President Sadi Carnot, the assassinations in Russia of the Czar and the Mayor of Moscow, and the Haymarket bombing in Chicago — as examples of how the great cause had been advanced.

"Before the proletariat can be mobilized to fight against a government, they must lose their trust in the government," she asserted. "A lazy liberal who expects his government to provide for his needs will still trust his government even when it fails miserably and incompetently to do so. A constipated conservative will still vote for a government that is tainted by yet another scandal. But the fundamental right and expectation of every citizen is that his government will protect him and his family. When a government fails in this most basic of duties, trust is destroyed. Therefore, our most effective weapon is the selective use of violence in a way that leads ordinary citizens to join our cause and overthrow the government."

Her logic might have been reasonable, but her moral position, as far as I was concerned, was highly distorted. Ends do not justify means, or at least that is what I believed. Sadly, it appeared that the crowd was much more in agreement with her than with me and she was given a loud round of applause, accompanied by shouts of "Bravo" when she ended her passionate speech.

"You say," said Holmes as we walked back to Baker Street, "that the two captains were together with Mrs. Lucy, the Princess Casamassima, at the reception."

I affirmed that the three of them had been there together.

"I am almost persuaded," admitted Holmes, "to regret that I declined the invitation to attend such an intolerable event. Almost, but not quite. I have some degree of confidence in your observations, and I thank you for them."

"And what now are your plans?" I asked.

"My suspicions have now shifted to this trio of anarchists," he said. "However, I do not yet have sufficient data on which to form a judgment. I must find a means of learning much more about them."

"Will you let slip the Company of Irregulars?" I asked.

"Under normal circumstances, I would, but there is an impediment in doing so. These Captains, as you have informed me, are here on a diplomatic mission and thus protected by diplomatic immunity. I must proceed with caution else I might unnecessarily create a row between England and France. The French are our good friends, whether we like them or not, and it just would not do to antagonize them."

"Yes, so what will you do?"

Holmes disappeared into his own mind for several minutes as we walked along Marylebone Road.

"I fear that I must confide in Lestrade and seek some sort of judicial approval before confronting two French diplomats. He will not be in his office tomorrow, as it will be Sunday, but might you be available first thing on Monday to accompany me to meet with him? Your services as my scribe are always appreciated."

I assured him that I would be eager to provide such assistance as I could, and we parted at the corner of Marylebone and Baker.

At eight o'clock on the Monday morning, I rang the bell at 221B. Holmes descended and together we took a cab down to the Embankment and the offices of Scotland Yard. Inspector Lestrade was at his desk in his cluttered, Spartan office and greeted us with a smile that bordered on a smirk.

"And to what do I owe the honor of meeting with England's only consulting detective and his Boswell this fine fall morning?"

We were seated, and Holmes thoroughly and patiently explained the reason for our visit.

"So, you are telling me you want to investigate these Frenchies, right? Didn't I tell you that they were who I suspected all along, right?"

"You did indeed, inspector," said Holmes.

"Good, glad you remembered that. Well, as far as I care, you can inspect the two of them all you want. In fact, you can jolly well go ahead and inspect them right down to their privates if you wish."

"I beg your pardon, Inspector?"

"You heard what I said, Holmes. If you want to strip the two boys from the Quai D'Orsay stark naked and inspect whatever you want, go ahead. Fact is, that's the way you'll find them right now."

Lestrade was now gloating openly.

"That's usually," he said, "what we do to corpses that are brought in here. Your Frenchies are in the morgue. *Aussi mort qu'une souris d'glise,* like they say in *Paarrie.*"

I was too shocked to correct his mangled metaphor. Holmes was likewise surprised but recovered immediately.

"Would you be so kind as to tell us what happened?" he asked.

"Oldest story in the book, Holmes. *Cherchez la femme,*" said Lestrade, and then he paused for dramatic effect.

"Please, Inspector?" asked Holmes.

"Not surprising, you know, Holmes, that it was the French who made up that rule, *cherchez la femme.* Seems those two *chasseurs* had both gone spoony over the same filly. Seems they were both besotted with a certain Princess and the competition got too heated. So, being French and given to thinking with their little heads instead of their big ones, if you know what I mean, they have a duel over her. Pistols at twenty paces in Hyde Park. Being as they are both military trained, they are good shots and send a slug into each other's hearts, and both end up dead. Their bodies were brought in early this morning. That's the French for you, Holmes. So, you can go and interrogate them all you want, but, like they say, dead men tell no tales."

"And the woman? This Princess?"

"She's here now too. Forbes has her in his office and is cross-questioning her at great length. If you ask me, he's taking his bloody good time about it seeing as she is a beauty to look at. But if you want to share in the pleasure, you can go and chat with her yourselves."

"Thank you, Inspector," said Holmes. "We will do just that. And I assume that you plan to have a report on this incident, yes?"

"Of course, I do. I will have a copy sent over to you when it is finished. Now, if you will excuse me, I still have a case to solve concerning who stole all those plans from the Admiralty. I hope you haven't forgotten about that, have you, Holmes?"

"Not at all, inspector. Not at all."

One of Lestrade's men, Constable Jerry, led us down the hall to Inspector Forbes's office. Responding to a respectful knock, Forbes opened the door. Jerry announced us and said that Lestrade's instructions were that Holmes was to be free to cross-question the woman. Then he turned around and walked away.

Forbes did not seem at all pleased with being interrupted. Once inside, it was obvious as to why. Sitting inside was the woman we had come to know as either Princess Casamassima, or Lucy Goldman. She was wearing a very tight dress that was slit up the side to permit both movement and the exposure of a perfectly formed calf and lower thigh. Although it was still early in the morning, she was perfectly coiffed, with every hair in place and just enough powder and paint to make her, yet again, dazzling.

"Oh my," she said. "I do declare, if it isn't the Baker Street boys. Lovely to see you again, Dr. Watson, and is this the famous Sherlock Holmes that I have read so much about? Well now, how do you do?"

She held out her hand to Holmes, who took it and made a very shallow bow toward her.

"I am honored to make your acquaintance. Do I call you Princess, or is it Mrs. Lucy?"

"Oh, my. Well now, a famous detective like Sherlock Holmes can call me whatever he wants. Had we met at the Langham, I am sure you would have called me Princess. Mind you, had you bothered, while in your awful disguise, to introduce yourself on Saturday morning at the Club, I am sure that just Lucy would have been fine. And do tell, Mr. Holmes, what did you think of my talk?"

Holmes was clearly not expecting that question and was momentarily nonplussed.

The lady continued. "Oh, please, Mr. Holmes. Do you not think it fair that if you have your Baker Street Irregulars spying on us that we should not be able to have agents of our own?" She laughed mischievously with that question, and I could plainly see why men might become so smitten with her that they would duel over the right to her affections.

"No doubt you are, madam," said Holmes. "However, I fear I am not interested in discussing the merits of our respective agents."

The smile vanished from the Princess's face.

"No, Mr. Holmes," she said softly and dropped her gaze to the floor. "I am sure you did not. Forgive me for trying to make light of a very sad situation. Failing to have a proper sense of decorum in tragic times is one of my besetting sins.

Please, forgive me. How may I assist you? I have already told my story to Scotland Yard. Shall I repeat it for you? Would that be useful, Mr. Holmes?"

"It would be very useful. Kindly do so, and please try not to omit any detail, no matter how seemingly unimportant."

The woman spoke in subdued tones and every so often paused to regain her composure.

"I met François and August several years ago in Paris. I had recently married my husband, the Prince of Aosta, and we were attending a function at the Italian Embassy in Paris. As tends to happen at such events, handsome young men are inevitably introduced to pretty young women. Do not ask me to explain why, I can only assure you that it happens, and I am honest enough to admit that my face is my fortune. I, in turn, introduced them to my husband and the three of them engaged in several business transactions that proved profitable. Again, do not ask me to explain, but mutually profitable business transactions between men inevitably lead them to think of each other as friends, and so the three of them became quite fond of each other."

"And the captains became fond of you?" asked Holmes, rather tactlessly.

"Yes, Mr. Holmes. That was also inevitable. We are speaking here of men, are we not? I can say before God, whoever he or she may be, that my behavior was honorable and I never deliberately led either of them to develop feelings toward me. I am not lacking in that skill when I have wished to use it, but I assure you that, as a happily married woman who had been very generously provided for by a wealthy husband, I had no interest in jeopardizing my fortune by treading on dangerous grounds.

"Nevertheless, both of them continued to express an interest in me and would send me, through private means, small gifts and flowers from time to time. I did not reciprocate and did my best to discourage their attentions, but they both persisted. Several months ago, it happened, by fate, that they were both posted to London at the same time as I was and, being good friends, we met regularly."

"I know why they were here," said Holmes. "Pray tell, why were you?"

"Did Dr. Watson not tell you? I am conducting research, paid for most kindly by my husband, into the comparable conditions of the poor in various European countries with the intent, I proudly acknowledge, of finding ways to help them organize themselves and throw off the yoke of capitalist oppression."

"A curious goal," said Holmes, "considering that your husband's fortune comes from his successful capitalist enterprises."

She smiled at him. "One of our writers, Mr. Kropotkin I believe it was, described some people as 'useful idiots.' My husband, bless his heart, has served wonderfully in that role."

"Has he now? Please, continue."

"Looking back, I should have been wiser. But I was alone in London, and they were wonderful and amusing company. We passed many lovely hours together at the theater or having dinners together. They were terribly attentive to me, but I brushed it off. I am used to excessive adoration from men. It was only in the past two weeks that I perceived that they had become quite competitive in seeking my attention. Each began to send me invitations to accompany them somewhere. I had often joined them for tea at their house in Belgravia, and on Wednesday last, while I was sitting in the parlor, I overheard them shouting at each other. They were saying things in French, which I do not speak at all well and could not understand, but I heard my name being uttered several times and I could tell that they were arguing about me.

"Last night, this note arrived. I was not able to make head nor tail of it then, but now, very sadly, it makes sense."

She handed a piece of paper to Holmes who read it and then handed it over to me. It was typewritten and ran:

```
By this time tomorrow, as fate will have
it, you will have only one of us to
choose from.
```

"I had no idea what it meant. It made no sense. I wondered if one of them had been called back to Paris, and they were going to flip a coin to decide which one it would be. I still cannot believe that they would fight a duel over me. I know they are French and all that, but it still seems pointless. And now it seems utterly insane. Two brilliant young men are dead, and for what? For a prize they could never receive anyway."

Here she appeared to lose her calm composure, lowered her head, and began to weep. When she had regained control of herself, she looked up at Holmes.

"I do not know what else there is, Mr. Holmes, that I could tell you. I last saw François and Autumn yesterday afternoon. The police came to my door nearly two hours ago now, and I came directly here with them. I have not gone down into the morgue to look at their bodies. I could bear to do that."

"Thank you, madam," said Holmes in a voice that bordered on compassion. "That is quite enough. Please accept my condolences. Their deaths were pointless, but, as you say, they are French, and these passions are in the blood. Good day, madam."

He rose and turned for the door. I stopped long enough to place a comforting hand on the shoulder of the princess. She looked up at me and, even with tears streaming down her face, she was radiantly beautiful.

"Come, Watson," said Holmes when I had caught up with him. "Let us pay a short visit to the morgue and see if it provides any clues."

We descended several flights of stairs into the cool of the police morgue. The fellows who attended to the place silently wheeled out the bodies of the two French captains. Both of them had been stripped of their clothing and their bodies washed.

"Are their garments available to be inspected?" asked Holmes.

"Sorry there, sir," came the answer from one of the attendants. "But a chap from the French embassy came by about forty-five minutes ago and collected up all their clothes, their shoes, watches, and the brace of pistols and the case and took them away."

"Without an opportunity to examine the clothing," said Holmes, "it is impossible to learn much about the distance from which the shots were fired. The wounds indicate that they were both using 52 caliber dueling pistols. The only remarkable thing about the wounds is that both of them were exceptionally accurate and hit the heart like a bull's eye."

"They were," I observed, "military men and some of those fellows were very good shots. I watched them at Maiwand pick off a nasty native warrior at a far greater distance than duelists stand from each other."

"Yes," said Holmes, "I suppose that is quite possible. If that is the case, then there is really nothing more we can learn here, and the story, for now, of how they came by their fates seems plausible."

Chapter Seven
Not Nothing

e parted. I took a cab back to my medical practice and Holmes one to who knows where. At about six o'clock I returned to my home near Little Venice and had the opportunity to chat with my dear wife, Mary, about the adventures of the day. As I was telling her about the Princess and the two French captains, her face took on a very odd look.

"What's wrong," I asked, as obviously something was vexing her.

"Nothing," she replied.

"No, darling," I said. "Clearly there is something bothering you."

"John, I said there was nothing."

Any man who has been married for more than a month has learned, usually the hard way, that when he asks his wife what is troubling her and twice receives the reply of "Nothing" that the true answer is more along the lines of "There is something bothering me. I do not want to talk about it. So stop asking."

I stopped asking.

When I returned to my home at the end of the following day, I could sense that Mary was still deeply troubled by something, but I knew that if I were to inquire, it would be at my peril. At the end of a pleasant supper, during which we chatted about the weather, the news, the new emporium that was about to be opened by Messrs. Marks and Spencer, and the events that had taken place during our day.

"I had a lovely time with Annie," said Mary. "We met in in Piccadilly and had a luncheon on Regent Street, and then we did some shopping."

"Excellent," I said. "And what did you buy?"

"Nothing, but we had an interesting chat."

"Excellent, and what did the two of you talk about?"

"Oh, nothing, really. But John, darling, would you mind asking Sherlock Holmes if Annie and I could have a brief meeting with him?"

I had not expected such a request.

"Of course, dearest, I can do that. What is it about?"

"Nothing."

"Dearest, it cannot be about nothing. What in the world would you and Annie want to talk to Holmes about?

"It is nothing, but if you are all that curious, I suggest you come with us, and you can find out."

I scribbled a note and went out to the pavement and hailed a page on a bicycle to run the note over to Baker Street. Just before my bedtime, a reply came back confirming that Holmes would be available to meet with Mary, Annie, and me the following day at five o'clock.

Mary, who still refused to talk with me about the reason for the meeting, met again for lunch with Annie Phelps. The two of them would find their own way to Baker Street, she assured me. I departed from my doctor's office in ample time to arrive early.

Mrs. Hudson greeted me warmly at the door and ushered me up the stairs where I waited alone. About ten minutes later, Sherlock Holmes walked in and almost immediately after him, my wife and Mrs. Annie Phelps.

"My dear Sherlock Holmes," began my wife once the three of us had been seated. "My husband informed me regarding the tragic deaths of the two French Captains the night before last."

Holmes merely nodded and gestured that she should continue.

"Mrs. Phelps and I are in agreement that whatever was the cause of their duel, it most certainly was not their competition for the attention of Princess Casamassima," said Mary.

"Absolutely not," said Annie Phelps. "Whatever was the

cause of their deaths, it could not possibly have been because of that woman."

"Holmes took the pipe out of his mouth. He was obviously intrigued. So was I.

"You have my attention. Please explain your reasons."

"It is a matter that is immediately perceived by any woman on earth," said Mary.

"Yes, any woman knows," confirmed Annie.

"When a woman," said Mary, "is in conversation with a man, she perceives, without fail, whether he is a gentleman who is addressing himself to her face..."

"Yes, her face," added Annie, "not her bodice."

"And if he is expressing any romantic interest, then he does so as a gentleman," said Mary.

"And not a knave," said Annie.

"Mrs. Phelps and I could tell that both of those French Captains were ravishing us with their eyes and treating us quite shamefully in their minds."

"It felt as if we were standing stark naked in front of them," said Annie.

"And all the while," said Mary, "they were standing beside a stunningly beautiful young woman who they appeared to know rather well."

"And they were," said Annie, "completely ignoring her and directing all their animal spirits toward us."

"She may as well," said Mary, "have been a block of ice. They had not a scrap of interest in her, and it is impossible that a few days later they would have acquired such a passion that they would kill each other over her."

"Yes, impossible," said Annie.

"Whatever was the cause of their duel, it most certainly was not over the Princess," said Mary.

"It must have been something else," said Annie, "for it certainly was not that woman."

Holmes looked intently at the two women, slowly moving his head back and forth and altering his gaze on first Mary and then Annie. He gave an appreciative nod each time.

"I have learned," he said, "that there are one or two matters where a woman has superior judgement to a man."

"Actually, Sherlock," said Mary, "I believe you mean to say that there are some matters in which women are never wrong, and men are entirely ignorant."

"Frankly," said Annie, "they are complete blockheads."

"And does this," asked Holmes, "appear to one of those times?"

In unison, both women replied in the affirmative.

Holmes lit his pipe and leaned back in his chair. "Watson," he said, turning to me. "Behind you on the table is today's post. I have not had the opportunity to view it yet, and the large brown envelope is most likely the report from Scotland Yard and the morgue. We will all see what they have to say about our two French captains. Would you mind handing it to me?"

I did as he had requested and could see the stamp of Scotland Yard on the largest piece.

He opened it and began to scan it quickly. Suddenly he threw it down on the coffee table.

"Those imbeciles!" he shouted. He leapt to his feet. "Ladies, kindly excuse us. Mrs. Watson, please hold your husband's supper for him until later this evening. Watson, come with me."

He was already walking out of the room. I bade my wife a quick good-bye and followed him down the stairs.

"Good Lord, Holmes," I shouted at him as he hailed a cab. "What in heaven's name is it? Where are we going?"

He gave the driver an address on a road behind Kensington Palace.

"There was no duel. They were both murdered."

I gasped. "Both of them? How can you tell?"

"I should have guessed when they simultaneously shot each other spot on in the heart. The likelihood of that happening is remote."

"But still possible," I replied.

"In total darkness?"

"What?"

"The police report said that the bodies were discovered by some bloke walking his dog in Hyde Park, just south of Bayswater. He found them at first light. He called the police immediately, and they were there in less than five minutes. The bodies were no longer warm to the touch, and the boys at the Yard agreed that they must have been dead for at least four hours. They were shot somewhere around midnight. No one schedules a duel between midnight and two o'clock in the morning when it is impossible to see who you are firing at. It is utterly absurd, even for the French."

It did seem a bit far-fetched when I thought it over.

"Where are we going now?"

"The French Embassy residences are along a street just behind Kensington Palace. That is where the two Captains have been living since they arrived in London."

The address was not far from Baker Street, and we arrived in less than ten minutes. The French diplomatic residences were immediately obvious by the Tri-Color flags hanging above several doorways in a parade of elegant row houses. The cab driver slowed down and looked for the specific house number that Holmes had given him. As we pulled up to the curb in front of that address, three people, an older couple and an attractive young woman, exited the house. I thought I had seen the three of them before.

"Were those service people at the reception at the Langham," I asked, wondering out loud.

"I was not there," said Holmes.

"Oh, yes, of course, you weren't. It is just that they looked familiar, that is all."

"You can ask about them when we go inside," said Holmes.

We walked up to the front door and were greeted by a very attractive red-haired woman in a maid's uniform. The bodice was cut rather low, and the skirt was somewhat on the short side, flared, and would be considered highly provocative at a house in Mayfair. But it was the French style, and as this was where they housed their diplomats, I assumed that it was in keeping with their ideas of fashion.

"Good evening, mademoiselle," said Holmes. "We are here on behalf of Scotland Yard to conduct the investigation into the duel."

The poor girl looked quite confused, and Holmes walked past her quickly. I followed him into the parlor.

"I did not know," I whispered to Holmes, "that we were sanctioned by Scotland Yard to inspect a diplomatic residence."

"We are not. Fortunately, the maid does not know that either. With the two Captains dead and gone, I suspect that the staff are in a sorry state of confusion. The girl seems pleasant enough. I suspect she is Irish and would be terrified if her mother and her priest knew that she was wearing a uniform like that. I will inspect the premises. Why don't you go and chat with her and see if she knows anything about what took place here on Sunday night?"

Holmes disappeared to the second floor, and I sought out the maid.

"Excuse me, miss," I said to the maid when I found her back in the kitchen. "Might I have a word with you?"

The poor girl looked awfully apprehensive and gave an awkward curtsy.

"Yes, sir. Of course, sir," she said.

"My name is Doctor John Watson ..."

That was all I had said before she gasped in astonishment.

"*The* Dr. Watson? The writer. Is that ... is that man with you ... Sherlock Holmes?" she asked.

"Yes, that is Sherlock Holmes."

She clasped her hands together under her chin, looked up at the ceiling and closed her eyes. Her lips were silently saying the words *thank you, Mother Mary* repeatedly. I made a mental note to pass on the Holmes the news that The Virgin appeared to be familiar with him.

"Oh, Dr. Watson, sir. This is an answer to my prayers. The past week here has been rotten, sir. I have been praying that The Virgin would come to my aid, and She has. She has sent Sherlock Holmes himself to help me."

I noticed a tear creeping down her freckled cheek, and her face was beaming with joy. I made another mental note to tell Holmes that he was not only known by the Virgin Mary but was now being sent as her emissary. I was not at all sure whether he would be pleased with his divine promotion.

"Please, miss," I said. "I assure you that Sherlock Holmes will do everything within his power to make sure that you and the other members of the staff here are safe. You could be a wonderful help to him, and he might even wish to thank you in one of the stories I write about him, if you would be so kind as to answer a few questions."

The dear girl's face lit up like a lamp, and she gasped again. "Indeed, sir? Would that be possible, sir? Why, of course, Dr. Watson, sir, if there is anything I can help you with, please just say so. I am at a loss for words to tell you how relieved I am that you and Mr. Holmes are here."

I was not sure that I knew anyone from Ireland, man or

woman, who was ever at a loss of words for any reason, but I proceeded with my questions.

"And what is your name, miss?" I asked.

"I would be Bridget O'Halloran, sir. From Galway, sir."

"Lovely to meet you, Miss Bridget. Please, my dear, there is no need to be afraid. But kindly tell me why it is that the last week has been so bad for you? Was it better before?"

"Before, sir, it was a bit of both good and bad. The wages we were paid were grand as was the food, seein' as they are French and all. It was no so bad before these two captains came and then it went manky. Those two were always bullin and they made the girls dress like prostitutes, and they were always puttin' their hands where they shouldn't be. The Douglas couple, fine Presbyters they were from Glasgow, they up and quit. That's when Captain François brought in Mr. and Mrs. Tangay to do the charring and the night watch. But we all knew it was on account of the daughter, Becky, that he hired her. That young bure is quite the feek. He was soon all over her like a randy bull on a heifer. Made Mrs. Tangay mad as a hornet, she was. Especially with his bein' a Frenchie.

"But that were not the worst of it. A week back there starts comin' around a dozen or so other bowsies and they are all yellin' and screamin' and calling the captains names. And that made the captains quite cheesed, and they take it out on those of us in service, they did."

"Pray, tell me, miss," I said. "Could you tell what these men who came around were angry about?"

"Well now, doctor, sir. In the first place, they were not all men. There were some women too, and they were screamin' like banshees as well. I have no languages other than English, sir, but it was like the Tower of Babel, sir. All sorts of tongues bein' screamed in, there was. What I could gather was that it all seemed to be about money, sir. Every day there was people I did not know comin' around, and this house has been hell and damnation for the past week, it has sir. And then we hear that the captains would be dead and we're not surprised, we're not, sir."

"Ah, is that so?" I said. "Did you know that the police are saying that the captains fought a duel over a woman and that is how they died."

Miss Bridget gave me a look of complete disbelief.

"If that is what the police believe, sir, then God help us all, sir. That is madness. Those coppers must be fluthered if that is what they think."

"And why do you say that, miss?"

"Those captains, sir, they were knaves when it come to women, sir. They didn't fight, they shared, and they thought it was all a lark, sir."

That was an interesting comment, I thought. It was not without reason that the French gave an entire new meaning to the word *ménage*. I decided to pursue another line of questions.

"Were there any other unusual visitors that came around in the past few weeks?"

"In this last week from hell, sir, no there weren't. Before that it was mostly other Frenchies, navy officers they looked like, sir, who came and got right ossified. Then a couple of months back there was the fuzzy-wuzzy fellow who came and did some repairs, but that was all."

"Pardon me, Miss Bridget, but what do you mean by a fuzzy-wuzzy?"

"Well, you know, sir. Like what the poet described – "a big black boundin' beggar with an 'errick 'ead of 'air." A bleedin' golliwogg, he was. One of those dark-skinned chaps from Africa. He came here for over two weeks and did the repairs."

"And might you remember the name of this fuzzy-wuzzy fellow?"

"His wagon, sir, had a name on it. It was Ibrahim and Company, it was, sir. On Acre Lane in Brixton was what was on the wagon, sir."

I continued to ask the girl several more questions and was sure that I had missed some data that Holmes would have sought out. I thanked her and wished her well.

"But what is to become of me, sir? With no one stayin' in this house, I'll be let go. And with the captains dead, who will give me a recommendation so that I can find a new position?"

"My dear girl," I said. "Here is my card. Send me a note, and I will be very happy to write a letter for you."

"Oh, sir. That would be right hatchet; it would sir. Every fine house in London knows your name, sir. Thank you, sir."

"And I will even add that you were very helpful to Sherlock Holmes."

I thought the dear girl was going to faint from joy. She

went so far as to throw her arms around me and place a sloppy wet kiss on my cheek. Had she not been scantily clad in her French maid's uniform, I might not have felt quite so uncomfortable with her display of affection.

Chapter Eight
Fuzzy-Wuzzy Wasn't, Was He?

I found Holmes and joined him in searching the remainder of the house. The entire place was neat and clean and stylish, as might have been expected of the French. Other than wardrobes that were overflowing with suits from Saville Row and military dress uniforms, paintings of naked women by French artists, and an abundance of busts of Napoleon, there was nothing out of the ordinary.

I passed on to Holmes the data I had acquired from Miss Bridget.

"It is highly unlikely," he said, "that it would be of any use to question the carousing French officers who visited here. And we do not know who the hostile visitors for the past week were yet. However, as we do know the name and location of the workman who had been coming by, we may as well start with him. Might you be free first thing tomorrow morning to meet me at Brixton Station? And it might be a good idea to bring your service revolver."

At eight the next day I met Holmes in Brixton, and together we walked around the corner to an address of a shop on Acre Road. There was a fellow there loading up a workman's closed wagon that bore the name we had been given, and it was unmistakably the man that Miss Bridget had described. His skin was coal black and his head of hair, pointing in all directions at once, was very striking. On his face were several symmetrical scar markings.

"Pardon me, sir," said Holmes. "Might we have a word with you?"

He looked up at us, gave a respectful nod and replied. "You wish to have a word with me, is it? And who might I ask is it that wishes to have this word?"

Like many of the African chaps who now live in London, he had a heavy accent and spoke as if he had a mouth full of wool.

"My name is Sherlock Holmes, and this is my colleague, Dr. Watson."

The African fellow's eyes widened, and a broad smile appeared on his face.

"Does Mr. Sherlock Holmes, the detective, wish to have a word with me? Then Mr. Hassan Ibrahim will be honored to speak with Mr. Sherlock Holmes. But am I able to do so this instant, you will ask. No, forgive me, Mr. Sherlock Holmes, but I am not. And why am I not? Because I am responding to an urgent call from a lady up in Chelsea whose ceiling has collapsed on her. And when will I become available to speak with Mr. Sherlock Holmes? In no more than one hour for that is all it will take to prop up her ceiling and make an estimate of the materials and time it will take make repairs. And will I be available after doing that? Yes, I will, and I shall meet you at The Rose on the bank of the Thames. Do they serve good food there for your breakfast, Mr. Holmes? No, sir, they do not. It is wretched, but it will have to do if you wish to speak with me this morning."

He said no more and jumped into his wagon, gave a wave to us, and a flick of his whip to his horse and moved off quickly.

I remarked on his unusual appearance. "He certainly looks the fuzzy-wuzzy does he not? Like one of those fierce Beja warriors from the Sudan that Kipling wrote about. Thought rather highly of them, he did."

"He could indeed be that," said Holmes. "Or he could be a promoter of pugilistic contests in America. I suppose that we shall find out when we meet him an hour from now."

As it was a pleasant, cool autumn morning, we elected to stroll up Lambeth Road to the pub to which Mr. Ibrahim had directed us. The Rose was situated along the embankment of the Thames and, except for the frequent blasts from the horns of the ships coming and going, it appeared to be a decent place with an agreeable view of the busy waterway. We had arrived in just under an hour and were relieved to see the workman's horse and wagon parked in front of the establishment. A sign on the pavement advertised a full English breakfast at a cost so reasonable that it had attracted quite a crowd of working men from the area. It should have been very easy to spot Mr. Ibrahim in such a crowd, but we entered and looked around for him, and he was not to be found.

"I do not think," I observed, "that he could disappear into a crowd like this in the daylight."

Holmes walked up to the bar and chatted briefly with the publican.

"Mr. Ibrahim is known here," said Holmes. "He is one of the regular customers. But the publican insists that he has not entered this morning."

"But that is his wagon outside," I said.

"Then we shall have to wait at the wagon," said Holmes.

Similar to any workman's wagon in London, it had a plank seat for the driver and behind that was an enclosed box of about ten feet in length and four in height. On the side was painted the name of Hasson Ibrahim and his address.

We waited for nearly fifteen minutes. Holmes is not blessed with the virtue of patience at times like this and was becoming agitated. Without any justification that I could discern, he moved to the back of the wagon and opened the doors. For a moment, he stood in silence and then I heard a long, slow sigh. I looked inside the wagon box and there, lying on his back on the floor, was the body of Mr. Ibrahim. He had been shot through the heart.

Holmes pulled out his police whistle and gave several loud blasts. A constable appeared almost instantly. Holmes provided him with whatever information we had on the poor fellow.

The constable conducted a cursory examination of the dead body and announced, "His pockets are empty. He's been robbed. It's happened before along the river, sir. They wait for a ship to blast on its horn, and then they shoot their victims. Unless you might be standing nearby, you cannot hear the gunshot over the horn. That's what happened here; you can be sure."

Soon several more police officers arrived, and again Holmes gave them such information as we could and again they concluded that the man was a victim of a robbery.

Once the police had loaded the body into their carriage, they departed. Holmes turned and began to walk slowly along the embankment toward the Lambeth Bridge.

"Wretched timing," I said as we walked north. "just as we were about to chat with the fellow, someone robs and shoots him."

Holmes positively glared at me. "Good lord, Watson. You cannot possibly be of so very little brain that you think that is what happened."

"I thought it was quite obvious. That's what the police constables thought as well, did they not?"

"Of course, because that is what they were supposed to think and they do not know any better. But I am disappointed that after all these years you could be so dull as to not see what was obvious."

"Are you saying," I asked, "that it was not robbery. You believe that it might have something to do with our meeting him?"

Holmes did not answer. He just glared at me again as if I were a dim-witted schoolboy.

"But how," I asked, "did they know he was going to meet with us?"

"He was being watched. Whoever was doing so also knew who we are and followed him. For some reason, it was imperative that he not speak to us."

"Then why," I asked, "did they not try to shoot *us*? That would have made more sense would it not?"

"Because they knew that you were armed."

"But how?"

"Because, Watson, in every one of your blasted stories, you insist on telling the world that I ask you to bring your service revolver and you always do so. That is how."

I pondered that for a few minutes as we continued to walk. The possibility that I had contributed somehow to the poor man's death was quite disturbing. Holmes, as he has done in the past, read my thoughts.

"Please, my friend," he said, "do not trouble yourself with feelings of remorse and guilt. It is neither your fault nor mine that the man knew too much. And in doing away with him, whoever is behind these murders has left us an irrefutable clue."

"Yes?"

"If it was necessary to kill him before he could speak to me, then there is something tied to his work at the French Embassy residence that must be kept secret. Perhaps we should return there at once and look again."

He hailed a cab, and we returned quickly to Kensington. Upon arrival at the French residences, I introduced Holmes to Miss Bridget O'Halloran. In spite of his hurried impatience, he took a moment to be gracious to her.

"Ah, yes, the lovely Irish lass from Galway. It is a pleasure to meet you, Miss O'Halloran."

The dear girl was quite flabbergasted, curtsied awkwardly, and blushed with embarrassment at being so warmly welcomed by someone as famous as Sherlock Holmes.

"Dr. Watson informs me," continued Holmes, "that you have provided very valuable information for our investigation and I am very grateful."

"Just doing my duty to try and help, sir," she replied.

"Excellent," said Holmes. "But now I have to ask you to tax your memory yet again and answer one or two more questions for me."

The poor thing looked quite terrified. "I will do what I can, sir. I am not a very well-schooled person, sir."

"And since when did schooling make a person honest and reliable?" said Holmes. "Now, please concentrate and tell me something. When the workman, the fellow you referred to as the fuzzy-wuzzy was here several weeks back, where in the house did he work and what did he do?"

"Sir, he did his work upstairs in the bedrooms. Shall I show you, Mr. Holmes, sir?"

"Yes, my dear, please do. That would be very helpful."

We ascended the stairs and followed Miss Bridget into the hallway.

"He did all his work up here, sir; a bit in each of the first three bedrooms and then quite some time in the fourth. But the doors were kept closed all the time, sir, so I cannot say what all he did, sir. I'm terribly sorry, sir."

"Nothing to be sorry for," said Holmes. "You have been exceptionally helpful. And when this case has been solved, and Dr. Watson writes the story and publishes it in the Strand, all the world will know that Miss Bridget O'Halloran, of Galway, was of invaluable assistance."

"Oh, sir. Just knowing that I was able to help Sherlock Holmes is a dream come true. And I will soon be away from this rotten place and into a new position. It is more than I could ever pray for."

Holmes graciously sent her back to her responsibilities, such as they were with the captains gone. He and I peered into the first bedroom.

"I went through this room quite thoroughly," he said, "and found nothing amiss. But I was searching the floors, closets, wardrobes, and the furniture. I was not looking at the ceilings. And that is to where I must needs turn my attention now."

"Why would you want to look at the ceilings?" I asked.

"There are scores of workmen all over London. Yet when a lady in Chelsea had an urgent problem with her ceiling, she called upon Mr. Ibrahim. It is, therefore, reasonable to assume that he has some reputation and expertise in the repair of ceilings, and that is also likely why he, of all available workmen in London, was called to do work here."

We entered the first bedroom, where Holmes went around the room with his walking stick held above his head and tap-tapped the ceiling. I could see that it had been freshly painted, but otherwise it appeared to be sound. We repeated the procedure on the second and third bedrooms. Again, the paint was fresh, but otherwise, there was nothing unusual.

On walking into the fourth bedroom, Holmes looked up and immediately turned around and re-entered the third bedroom and gazed one more time at that ceiling. He returned and looked up again at the ceiling of the fourth room.

"Look, Watson," he said.

"At what?"

"This ceiling is a full nine inches lower than the one in the bedroom beside it. Yet the floors are uniform in height throughout. This ceiling has been dropped and replaced, and I suspect it was done recently."

He took a few steps around the room and poked at the ceiling with his stick. There was a distinct hollow sound from it. He continued to tap all over the ceiling and then stopped at the place below where it met the far wall.

"Watson, kindly take a look at the bottom edge of the coving. Do you see anything unusual?"

I looked and, although it was difficult to make out, it looked as if there was a small rounded ridge running along the lower edge of the coving. I noted my observation to Holmes.

"Precisely," he said. "Now, excuse me for a minute. I recollect seeing that there was a ladder in the basement of this house. Please wait here whilst I go and get it."

He departed, returning a few minutes later, bearing an eight-foot ladder. Leaning it up against the center of the far wall he clambered up and, at the top, pulled out his glass and looked carefully at the lower edge of the coving. He then put the glass back in his pocket and used a pen knife to scrape at the small ridge.

"There is," he said, "a finely crafted piano hinge running the length of this wall, attaching the coving to the lath. It is made of brass but has been painted over so that it is barely visible. Somehow this entire stretch of coving must fold down."

"That is most peculiar," I said.

"And very ingenious," he said. "Had the killers not done away with Mr. Ibrahim, I would not have been directed to look here."

He descended the ladder, moved it to the corner of the room, and climbed back up.

"Ah, yes. There it is," he said.

"There what is?"

"A small angle bracket straddling the corner, holding this hinged coving to the adjacent one. I believe that with my knife I shall be able to unscrew it and lower the length of coving. As I do so, Watson, could you please stand below me, and use your stick to keep the coving in place, whilst I then undo the far end and we lower the entire length of it?"

I did so, and held my stick against the coving whilst

Holmes slowly and carefully undid the bracket holding it in place. Once he has removed the bracket, he quickly scampered down the ladder and moved it to the other corner of the wall. Again, he climbed up and unscrewed a bracket holding the length of coving in place.

"Our poor Mr. Ibrahim was quite the craftsman," said Holmes as he perched at the top of the ladder and worked. "These brackets have been countersunk into precisely cut hollows and painted over so that they are almost invisible. Now ... the bracket is off. Slowly, Watson, lower your stick at the same time as I let down my end. If I am not mistaken, the entire length of the coving will fold down exposing a cavity above the ceiling."

Together, we lowered the coving, which fell away from the ceiling, held in place by the long piano hinge that ran the length of it. From where I stood on the floor, I could see nothing in the space that it now exposed, but Holmes exulted.

"Ah ha! A wide, flat opening. Just the right size for holding large technical drawings. Let me move the ladder and see if I can reach inside one of them."

Again, he came down the ladder and now moved it back to the middle of the wall and once again climbed up. This time he was able to reach his hand around the suspended coving and into the cavity above the new ceiling. The look that took over his face announced that he had found his hidden treasure. Slowly, he extracted a wide sheet of paper and carefully handed it down to me. Even to my untrained eye, it was clear that I was looking at a detailed technical plan for a large boat. We had found the missing plans for Britain's ships of the line.

I excused myself for a few minutes, scribbled out two quick notes to Inspector Lestrade and Percy Phelps and called upon the eager-to-please Miss Bridget to find a page and send them off forthwith. I then returned to the fourth bedroom and assisted Holmes as he extracted page after large page of plans and handed them down to me. Eventually, there was a pile several inches high of over-sized sheets of paper on the floor of the room, every page showing the detailed plans for another portion of one of Great Britain's latest ships.

Percy and Lestrade both arrived in half an hour, and expressed enormous relief upon seeing the plans. I could not help but remember Percy's similar joy and relief when he uncovered his breakfast plate seven years ago.

"Must hand it to you, Holmes," said Lestrade. "It appears that you have done it again. I have no doubt that these could have been sold for thousands and thousands of pounds to our enemies. Even our allies would have gladly paid for them. The Americans alone would have offered a king's ransom."

"Once again, Mr. Holmes," said a beaming Percy Phelps, "you have saved my life and my career. I do not know what I can ever do to show my gratitude and repay you."

Within the hour, several constables had arrived, and they carefully packaged up the trove of plans and placed them inside a police carriage, for safe return to the Admiralty.

I suggested to Holmes that I treat him to a fine dinner to celebrate the successful conclusion of the case. He seemed somewhat distracted and demurred. I decided to leave it a few days, and then call him over to join Mary and me in a quiet celebration.

Chapter Nine
The Big Match Day

The following Saturday morning, Percy and Annie Phelps, my wife, Mary, and I and Sherlock Holmes gathered in our home near Little Venice to acknowledge the brilliant work of our most unusual friend. We enjoyed a delectable full English breakfast that, notwithstanding the opinion of the unfortunate Mr. Ibrahim, was as fine a cuisine as could be imagined by a true son or daughter of our green and pleasant land.

"Please. Mr. Holmes," said Annie Phelps, "you must explain to us how it was you so brilliantly put it all together. Please, do tell us."

"I would refrain from calling anything brilliant when a

good man and diligent craftsman such as Hassam Ibrahim ends up dead. And I believe that you now know as much as I do. It was apparent from what the two of you told me, that the Captains could not possibly have fought a duel over Princess Casamassima, or Miss Lucy, or whoever that consummate actress is. It is most likely that the Captains were not in the least interested in La Révolution but intent only on lining their own pockets, and that their fervently committed comrades eventually realized that they were merely dupes who were being deprived of their money. They then reacted, as all anarchists are prone to do, and shot those who betrayed the cause."

"But do you know who amongst them it was?" asked Percy.

"No," said Holmes, "and I shall leave that to Lestrade and his men. They have finally taken several of the members of the Club Automatiste into custody and are leaning heavily on them to inform on their comrades. Scotland Yard is quite skilled in doing such things, and I expect that they will succeed."

"Yes, I expect they will," I said. "However, how was it that the Frenchies managed to steal the plans in the first place?"

I directed this question more toward Percy than Holmes, and it was he who replied.

"In truth, John, I do not know. The captains must somehow have secured a key to the vault room and come in late at night and spirited the plans away. I have immediately removed the locks and had the chaps at Chubbs install the latest and best locks and combination dials available. Nothing like this must ever take place again."

Holmes had been quietly puffing on his pipe, and now he turned to Percy.

"And are you quite certain that all of the plans that were stolen are now returned and secured?"

"Oh yes. We have them all back. At least, that is, all the ones that really matter to us."

Holmes took the pipe from his mouth and gave a look to Percy.

"What do you mean 'the ones that mattered to us?' Were they all returned or not?"

"All of our ships of the line, and all the large merchant marine plans are back. The only ones that are still missing are the ones for the Woolwich ferries. Can you imagine that? They had access to our battleships, and all they kept were a couple of ferry boats. Frankly, we do not care if Germany or Italy or even America has those plans. They are welcome to them. They have no real value to the Admiralty."

"Then why, sir, "said Holmes, "would anyone want to steal them?"

"It beats me," said Percy. "These boats are quite new, but all they do is churn their way back and forth across the Thames, taking working chaps to the Docklands or the Royal Arsenal. On a weekday, they carry several score of passengers and, on the weekends, they are almost empty."

"Except," I said, "on a big match day."

"What, Watson," said Holmes, "do you mean by a 'big match day?'"

Every sportsman in London would have understood what I had just said, but I had to explain it to Holmes.

"Twice in the season, the team from the Royal Arsenal, who are on the south shore, play The Irons, the team from the Thames Iron Works, who are on the north shore. It is quite the occasion. Great rivals they are and several thousand fans come and watch and cheer. Depending on which team has home field for the game, either the Arsenal fans will cross over to the north, or the Irons will have to cross to the south. The ferries are packed on those days."

Holmes's face had suddenly become pale. "And when," he asked, "is the next big match?"

"This afternoon," I said. "Starts at two forty-five. It has been in all the sporting pages of the press. It is being played in the Boleyn Grounds and the Arsenals and their fans will all be crossing. The stadium holds over 35,000. Half of them will be from Arsenal and most of them will cross in the ferries. Promises to be quite the spectacle. All those football fans make for quite the party coming and going and in the stands."

"Good Lord," whispered Holmes.

I looked over at him and was alarmed. I have observed Sherlock Holmes as he reacted to countless circumstances. Only on one or two occasions in the past had I seen the horrifying look that I now saw on his face. He had paled and was trembling. He was terrifyingly afraid.

Chapter Ten
A Sinking Feeling

hen he sprang to his feet. "Watson!" he shouted at me. "Come. Now!" He was already rushing out the door. I followed him out to the pavement where he was screaming for a cab.

"Scotland Yard!" he shouted to the cabbie. "As fast as you can go!"

He kept his head leaning out of the cab window and shouting directions to the cab driver as we galloped south on Edgeware Road, then across Oxford Street and down through central London until we reached the offices of Scotland Yard on the Embankment. Upon reaching the Yard, he leapt from the cab and rushed inside the building.

"LESTRADE!" he shouted as loud as I have ever heard his voice. The officers at the desk, who all knew him, were alarmed.

"Lestrade!" he shouted again, and then again.

Inspector Lestrade emerged and appeared about to rebuke Holmes for his highly unacceptable outburst, but then he saw what I had seen on Holmes's face. He saw the unmistakable fear and terror.

"Good heavens, Holmes. What is it?"

"We need a dozen of your men to the Woolwich ferries. At once!" He was screaming at the inspector.

For a brief second, Lestrade hesitated and then must have realized, as I had, that Holmes was deadly serious and he began shouting orders. In less than a minute, a dozen constables had emerged from the office and gathered at the front desk.

"Your fastest police carriages," commanded Holmes. "To the Woolwich ferry. South shore. They used the plans to put a bomb on board."

The look on the faces of the policemen made it clear that, being sportsmen all, they knew about the big match and the thousands of fans who would be crossing. A look of horror came across Lestrade's face, and he also began to shout at his men to move faster. Two large police carriages were quickly summoned, and we clambered in. Off we went with bells clanging and whistles blowing.

"Are you certain?" demanded Lestrade, shouting at Holmes as we galloped along the Embankment and across Blackfriars Bridge.

"No!" Holmes shouted back at him. "But if I am right, a disaster is about to take place. If I am wrong, we can live with the embarrassment. Do you want to risk that, Inspector?"

Lestrade stared at Holmes briefly and then stuck his head out the window and screamed at the driver to give more speed.

The time was already well past noon, and the ferries would be working at full capacity, transporting the raucous football fans across the Thames. Even at a full gallop, it would take us close to thirty minutes to get all the way to the docks in Woolwich. Fortunately, it was a Saturday, and the traffic on Lower Road and Woolwich Road was light, and the carts and wagons scampered out of the way when they heard the clamor of the police carriages. The powerful horses thundered past shops and houses and small buildings. Londoners standing on the pavements stopped where they were and looked at us in wonder as we sped past them.

The carriage rocked and bounced as we tore along the streets. After what seemed an eternity, the traffic circle in front of the ferry docks came into view. There was a queue of people, several thousand of them, snaking their way around it and up to the docks. Being football fans, they were already singing and bellowing their cheers and were no doubt well into their cups even before arriving at the stadium.

We had to slow down and force the crowds to part as we entered the ferry docks. One boat was just pulling in to the dock, making its way back from the north side of the Thames. It appeared to be almost empty.

"That's the *Gordon* coming back from the Pier Road

dock," Lestrade commanded his men. "Do not let anyone get on it after it docks and discharges its passengers. And get the captain and crew off of it!"

As we pulled up closer to the boarding ramps, we could see that the second ferry, the *Duncan* had just pulled away. Its great paddle wheel was churning up the water as it surged out into the open expanse of the Thames. It was utterly jammed with passengers. Not an inch of railing was vacant as the loyal Arsenal fans leaned against the rails and enjoyed the brisk fall breeze on the river.

If there was a bomb on board and it exploded when the ferry was in the middle of the river, a thousand lives could be lost. The boat had to be stopped.

One of the constables, who was now fully apprised of the danger, spotted a small private ferry at a dock to the left of the main pier. He and a fellow officer were already running toward it, and soon they had commandeered it and pulled up to the boarding area. The owner of it did not look at all happy, especially when the officers ordered his passengers off and Holmes, Lestrade, two constables, and I boarded.

"Catch up to the Duncan!" ordered Lestrade. "Now get moving. On the double."

The driver did as ordered and soon the sleek smaller craft was cutting its way through the chop of the river. The Thames at Woolwich is half a mile wide, and the Duncan was already one hundred yards out and into deep water. But we were moving quickly and were soon alongside it and signaling to the bridge. The captain understood our orders and slowly began to turn the large ferry around and head back to the dock on the south side of the river.

At first, the passengers were confused by what was happening, but then as it became obvious that they were being taken back from whence they came, the mood became rather ugly. They had already stood in line for up to two hours to get on the boat, and were not pleased with being returned. The shouts and jeers from both the lower and upper decks were not at all respectful of the officers of Scotland Yard. As soon as the Duncan reached its berth on the south dock, several constables ran on board and started shouting at the passengers to disembark. They were not particularly cooperative about doing so. Once on the dock, they were pushed back into the crowd who had been prohibited from boarding the Gordon.

By now there must have been several thousand football fans thronging the end of the dock, and the police were hard-pressed to keep them back from the boats. There are few things in British life that are more unpredictable than a throng of football fans, but one of them has to be the same throng who are quickly seeing that they will not even get to the stadium to watch the match. The screams and invective coming from them was frightening, and I feared that they could easily break into an unruly mob who might attempt to storm the boats.

And that is what happened. One of the louts who was likely quite drunk shouted, "To the boats!" and started running past the thin blue line of constables. He was immediately followed by a hundred more, and they began stampeding down the dock back to the boarding ramps.

Then they stopped.

An enormous explosion blew out of the side of the Duncan at midships, just at the water line. Debris came hurtling toward the crowds, and the smoke and flares were terrifying. The crowd retreated in stunned silence. A gaping hole in the boat appeared after the smoke had cleared. We watched as the ferry quickly took on water and began to list. Soon the entire boat was sinking into the water. The tide was out, and there was only a few feet of clear water between the underside of the boat and the sand on the river bottom. Within ten minutes the Duncan had sunk down and was resting on the mud, water washing over the lower deck. Had it been out on the river, it would have quickly become fully submerged. The crowds, who were looking on in horror, could see that they would have drowned had they not been forced off the boat.

Unfortunately, the closest bridge across the Thames was all the way back past the Isle of Dogs and to the Tower. There was no possible way that several thousand fans could get back there and then run along the north side in time to see more than the few final minutes of the match.

Lestrade seized the occasion and took a bull horn from out of one of the police carriages. He walked confidently toward the fans.

"Now hear this!' he shouted. "On order of Scotland Yard, the match between Royal Arsenal and the Irons will be postponed until tomorrow afternoon. All of you now, get along. Enjoy your day. Nothing more to see here. The match will take place tomorrow."

A roar of approval went up from the crowd, and someone

led a cheer for the police. It was followed by several more cheers, and the fans slowly turned and began to make their way back into the neighborhoods and pubs of South Woolwich and the other sections of Greenwich.

The three of us surveyed the damage to the ferry. It was lying on the shallow flats that bordered the docks and, to my untrained eye, it looked as if the damage could be repaired within a couple of months and the boat put back into service.

"What about the other boat," I asked. "Might there be a bomb on board the Gordon as well?"

"Most likely not," said Holmes. "Had there been it would have gone off by now, and since only one of the boats at a time was crossing with a full load of passengers, there would have been no point in placing two bombs. Once the first bomb had gone off, the other boat would never have loaded any more people. But for good measure, the constables should do a full search."

Lestrade agreed, and the constables took the better part of the next hour to search the Gordon from stem to stern. No dynamite was found.

The big match was postponed and played the following day. The near-disaster of the drowning of over a thousand fans of the Royal Arsenal team was replaced with the actual disaster of their resounding defeat at the hands of the Irons.

Over the course of the next week, the press ran stories and pictures of the bombing of the Woolwich ferry. Scotland Yard was universally praised for its brilliant actions in discovering the anarchist plot and preventing a terrible tragedy. A team of constables, led by Inspectors Lestrade and Forbes rounded up most of the members of the Club Autonomie and put them through the third degree. Several of them agreed to inform on their fellow comrades, and it was generally acknowledged that the two French naval captains had been eliminated because of their greedy efforts to use the cause and the selling of the plans for their own personal gain.

The woman known either as Lucy Goldman or Princess Casamassima was understood to be the ringleader of the violent plot to sink the Woolwich ferry. A notice for her arrest had been circulated throughout England, but it was reported that on the day following the failed bombing, a woman matching her description was observed on the ferry to Calais. She had escaped.

On the Friday of that week, Holmes, Lestrade, Percy and I met in a pub near the Admiralty offices to conduct our post-mortem of the case. Lestrade, understandably, was quite jovial but, to his credit, gave credit where it was due.

"Not sure at all what we are going to do with you, Holmes," he said between large gulps of his ale. "It just won't do to have you barging into diplomatic residences claiming that you are acting on behalf of Scotland Yard. But we admit that had you not done that we would still be searching for all those plans and still fishing bodies of football fans out of the Thames."

"I would have thought," said Holmes, smiling slyly, "that there are days when Scotland Yard would not have minded at all if there were a thousand fewer football fans alive and roaming the streets and ferries of London."

Lestrade thought that was quite funny and laughed loudly. Fortunately, he did not have his mouth full of ale at the time.

"Right," he said. "But you will have to come up with a more elegant way of helping us get rid of them."

"And you, Mr. Phelps," Lestrade said, turning to Percy, who had not joined in the laughter and appeared rather sullen. "Got your locks changed, I hear."

Percy shrugged his shoulders and replied. "Yes, we did. Although it seems to have been unnecessary."

"Well then," continued Lestrade, slapping Percy on the back, "we hope you're doing a better job of investigating visiting French diplomats before allowing them a chance to pirate your vaults."

"I suppose we could do that," he said. "But again, it is not necessary."

"Not necessary?" said Lestrade. "What do you mean, not necessary? They stole you blind."

"No sir, they did not. They only purchased the plans with the intent of selling them on to various foreign powers. The protection I will have to take, I regret, is from the actions of my dear, loving but awfully naïve wife."

The three of us looked at him in disbelief.

"Mr. Phelps," said Holmes. "Kindly explain yourself."

"My secretary, Mr. Charles Gorot, has not come in for work this entire week. His residence is vacant. We received a report that he was seen on Sunday afternoon on the Calais ferry. He was standing by the rail with his protective arm around a woman, a beautiful woman who was said to be ... dazzling."

Historical and Other Notes

The final years of the Victorian era were full of international intrigue, espionage, and the actions of anarchists. One September 15, 1894, Martain Bourdin, a French anarchist living in London, died while carrying a bomb near the Greenwich Observatory. The accounts of the incident vary but are more or less as described in the story, including the borrowed library book on how to make a bomb, but not including the stolen plans.

London was a city of refuge for European anarchists from throughout Europe and they met at the Club Autonomie. The assassinations and bombings carried out by anarchists and noted in the story took place as described. The widely admired (among anarchists) Communard, Mme. Louise Michel, lived in exile in London from 1890 to 1895.

The shipyards of England were highly productive during these years, turning out the world's most advanced ships of war for the British Navy. Sir Ughtred Kay-Shuttleworth (his actual name) served as Parliamentary Secretary to the Navy during the latter part of the 1890s.

Marks and Spencer opened their first store during the weeks that this story takes place. The debate on the accumulation of horse manure also appeared in the press at this time.

Many of today's great football clubs began as recreational programs for men working in the massive factories of England. The Thames Iron Works formed a team initially called "The Irons." It changed its name to West Ham, but the team crest continues to this day to show the crossed hammers of the ironworkers. The workers at the Royal Arsenal formed the team that now plays under the name of Arsenal. Both teams began and continue to play in the neighborhoods of North and South Woolwich.

The Woolwich ferries, the Duncan and the Gordon, were launched in the late years of the nineteenth century and crossed back and forth across the Thames for several decades. They were never bombed.

The character and description of Princess Casamassima is fictional, but has been borrowed from the novel by Henry James in which she is a supporter of anarchists, and dazzling.

About the Author

In May of 2014 the Sherlock Holmes Society of Canada – better known as The Bootmakers – announced a contest for a new Sherlock Holmes story. Although he had no experience writing fiction, the author submitted a short Sherlock Holmes mystery and was blessed to be declared one of the winners. Thus inspired, he has continued to write new Sherlock Holmes Mysteries since and is on a mission to write a new story as a tribute to each of the sixty stories in the original Canon. He currently writes from Toronto, the Okanagan, and Manhattan.

More Historical Mysteries

by Craig Stephen Copland
www.SherlockHolmesMystery.com

 ***Studying Scarlet.*** Starlet O'Halloran, a fabulous mature woman, who reminds the reader of Scarlet O'Hara (but who, for copyright reasons cannot actually be her) has arrived in London looking for her long-lost husband, Brett (who resembles Rhett Butler, but who, for copyright reasons, cannot actually be him). She enlists the help of Sherlock Holmes. This is an unauthorized parody, inspired by Arthur Conan Doyle's *A Study in Scarlet* and Margaret Mitchell's *Gone with the Wind.*

 ***The Sign of the Third.*** Fifteen hundred years ago the courageous Princess Hemamali smuggled the sacred tooth of the Buddha into Ceylon. Now, for the first time, it is being brought to London to be part of a magnificent exhibit at the British Museum. But what if something were to happen to it? It would be a disaster for the British Empire. Sherlock Holmes, Dr. Watson, and even Mycroft Holmes are called upon to prevent such a crisis. This novella is inspired by the Sherlock Holmes mystery, *The Sign of the Four.*

 A Sandal from East Anglia. Archeological excavations at an old abbey unearth an ancient document that has the potential to change the course of the British Empire and all of Christendom. Holmes encounters some evil young men and a strikingly beautiful young Sister, with a curious double life. The mystery is inspired by the original Sherlock Holmes story, *A Scandal in Bohemia.*

The Bald-Headed Trust. Watson insists on taking Sherlock Holmes on a short vacation to the seaside in Plymouth. No sooner has Holmes arrived than he is needed to solve a double murder and prevent a massive fraud diabolically designed by the evil Professor himself. Who knew that a family of devout conservative churchgoers could come to the aid of Sherlock Holmes and bring enormous grief to evil doers? The story is inspired by *The Red-Headed League.*

A Case of Identity Theft. It is the fall of 1888 and Jack the Ripper is terrorizing London. A young married couple is found, minus their heads. Sherlock Holmes, Dr. Watson, the couple's mothers, and Mycroft must join forces to find the murderer before he kills again and makes off with half a million pounds. The novella is a tribute to A Case of Identity. It will appeal both to devoted fans of Sherlock Holmes, as well as to those who love the great game of rugby.

The Hudson Valley Mystery. A young man in New York went mad and murdered his father. His mother believes he is innocent and knows he is not crazy. She appeals to Sherlock Holmes and, together with Dr. and Mrs. Watson, he crosses the Atlantic to help this client in need. This new storymystery was inspired by *The Boscombe Valley Mystery.*

The Mystery of the Five Oranges. A desperate father enters 221B Baker Street. His daughter has been kidnapped and spirited off the North America. The evil network who have taken her has spies everywhere. There is only one hope – Sherlock Holmes. Sherlockians will enjoy this new adventure, inspired by The Five Orange Pips and Anne of Green Gables.

The Man Who Was Twisted But Hip. France is torn apart by The Dreyfus Affair. Westminster needs Sherlock Holmes so that the evil tide of anti-Semitism that has engulfed France will not spread. Sherlock and Watson go to Paris to solve the mystery and thwart Moriarty. This new mystery is inspired by, _The Man with the Twisted Lip_, as well as by _The Hunchback of Notre Dame._

The Adventure of the Blue Belt Buckle. A young street urchin discovers a man's belt and buckle under a bush in Hyde Park. A body is found in a hotel room in Mayfair. Scotland Yard seeks the help of Sherlock Holmes in solving the murder. The Queen's Jubilee could be ruined. Sherlock Holmes, Dr. Watson, Scotland Yard, and Her Majesty all team up to prevent a crime of unspeakable dimensions. A new mystery inspired by _The Blue Carbuncle._

The Adventure of the Spectred Bat. A beautiful young woman, just weeks away from giving birth, arrives at Baker Street in the middle of the night. Her sister was attacked by a bat and died, and now it is attacking her. A vampire? The story is a tribute to _The Adventure of the Speckled Band_ and like the original, leaves the mind wondering and the heart racing.

The Adventure of the Engineer's Mom. A brilliant young Cambridge University engineer is carrying out secret research for the Admiralty. It will lead to the building of the world's most powerful battleship, The Dreadnaught. His adventuress mother is kidnapped and he seeks the help of Sherlock Holmes. This new mystery is a tribute to _The Engineer's Thumb._

The Adventure of the Notable Bachelorette. A snobbish nobleman enters 221B Baker Street demanding the help in finding his much younger wife – a beautiful and spirited American from the West. Three days later the wife is accused of a vile crime. Now she comes to Sherlock Holmes seeking to prove her innocence. This new mystery was inspired *The Adventure of the Noble Bachelor.*

The Adventure of the Beryl Anarchists. A deeply distressed banker enters 221B Baker St. His safe has been robbed, and he is certain that his motorcycle-riding sons have betrayed him. Highly incriminating and embarrassing records of the financial and personal affairs of England's nobility are now in the hands of blackmailers. Then a young girl is murdered. A tribute to *The Adventure of the Beryl Coronet.*

The Adventure of the Coiffured Bitches. A beautiful young woman will soon inherit a lot of money. She disappears. Another young woman finds out far too much and, in desperation seeks help. Sherlock Holmes, Dr. Watson and Miss Violet Hunter must solve the mystery of the coiffured bitches, and avoid the massive mastiff that could tear their throats. A tribute to *The Adventure of the Copper Beeches.*

The Silver Horse, Braised. The greatest horse race of the century, will take place at Epsom Downs. Millions have been bet. Owners, jockeys, grooms, and gamblers from across England and America arrive. Jockeys and horses are killed. Holmes fails to solve the crime until… This mystery is a tribute to *Silver Blaze* and the great racetrack stories of Damon Runyon.

The Box of Cards. A brother and a sister from a strict religious family disappear. The parents are alarmed, but Scotland Yard says they are just off sowing their wild oats. A horrific, gruesome package arrives in the post, and it becomes clear that a terrible crime is in process. Sherlock Holmes is called in to help. A tribute to *The Cardboard Box*.

The Yellow Farce. Sherlock Holmes is sent to Japan. The war between Russia and Japan is raging. Alliances between countries in these years before World War I are fragile, and any misstep could plunge the world into Armageddon. The wife of the British ambassador is suspected of being a Russian agent. Join Holmes and Watson as they travel around the world to Japan. Inspired by *The Yellow Face*.

The Stock Market Murders. A young man's friend has gone missing. Two more bodies of young men turn up. All are tied to The City and to one of the greatest frauds ever visited upon the citizens of England. The story is based on the true story of James Whitaker Wright and is inspired by, *The Stock Broker's Clerk*. Any resemblance of the villain to a certain American political figure is entirely coincidental.

The Glorious Yacht. On the night of April 12, 1912, off the coast of Newfoundland, one of the greatest disasters of all time took place – the Unsinkable Titanic struck an iceberg and sank with a horrendous loss of life. The news of the disaster leads Holmes and Watson to reminisce about one of their earliest adventures. It began as a sailing race and ended as a tale of murder, kidnapping, piracy, and survival through a tempest. A tribute to *The Gloria Scott*.

A Most Grave Ritual. In 1649, King Charles I escaped and made a desperate run for Continent. Did he leave behind a vast fortune? The patriarch of an ancient Royalist family dies in the courtyard, and the locals believe that the headless ghost of the king did him in. The police accuse his son of murder. Sherlock Holmes is hired to exonerate the lad. A tribute to *The Musgrave Ritual.*

The Spy Gate Liars. Dr. Watson receives an urgent telegram telling him that Sherlock Holmes is in France and near death. He rushes to aid his dear friend, only to find that what began as a doctor's house call has turned into yet another adventure as Sherlock Holmes races to keep an unknown ruthless murderer from dispatching yet another former German army officer. A tribute to *The Reigate Squires.*

The Cuckold Man Colonel James Barclay needs the help of Sherlock Holmes. His exceptionally beautiful, but much younger, wife has disappeared and foul play is suspected. Has she been kidnapped and held for ransom? Or is she in the clutches of a deviant monster? The story is a tribute not only to the original mystery, *The Crooked Man*, but also to the biblical story of King David and Bathsheba.

The Impatient Dissidents. In March 1881, the Czar of Russia was assassinated by anarchists. That summer, an attempt was made to murder his daughter, Maria, the wife of England's Prince Alfred. A Russian Count is found dead in a hospital in London. Scotland Yard and the Home Office arrive at 221B and enlist the help of Sherlock Holmes to track down the killers and stop them. This new mystery is a tribute to *The Resident Patient.*

The Grecian, Earned. This story picks up where *The Greek Interpreter* left off. The villains of that story were murdered in Budapest, and so Holmes and Watson set off in search of "the Grecian girl" to solve the mystery. What they discover is a massive plot involving the re-birth of the Olympic games in 1896 and a colorful cast of characters at home and on the Continent.

The Three Rhodes Not Taken. Oxford University is famous for its passionate pursuit of learning. The Rhodes Scholarship has been recently established and some men are prepared to lie, steal, slander, and, maybe murder, in the pursuit of it. Sherlock Holmes is called upon to track down a thief who has stolen vital documents pertaining to the winner of the scholarship, but what will he do when the prime suspect is found dead? A tribute to *The Three Students*.

A Scandal in Trumplandia. NOT a new mystery but a political. The story is a parody of the much-loved original story, *A Scandal in Bohemia*, with the character of the King of Bohemia replaced by you-know-who. If you enjoy both political satire and Sherlock Holmes, you will get a chuckle out of this new story.

Sherlock and Barack. This is NOT a new Sherlock Holmes Mystery. It is a Sherlockian research monograph. Why did Barack Obama win in November 2012? Why did Mitt Romney lose? Pundits and political scientists have offered countless reasons. This book reveals the truth - The Sherlock Holmes Factor. Had it not been for Sherlock Holmes, Mitt Romney would be president.

From The Beryl Coronet to Vimy Ridge. This is NOT a New Sherlock Holmes Mystery. It is a monograph of Sherlockian research. This new monograph in the Great Game of Sherlockian scholarship argues that there was a Sherlock Holmes factor in the causes of World War I... and that it is secretly revealed in the *roman a clef* story that we know as *The Adventure of the Beryl Coronet*.

Reverend Ezekiel Black—'The Sherlock Holmes of the American West'—Mystery Stories.

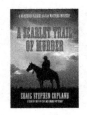

A Scarlet Trail of Murder. At ten o'clock on Sunday morning, the twenty-second of October, 1882, in an abandoned house in the West Bottom of Kansas City, a fellow named Jasper Harrison did not wake up. His inability to do was the result of his having had his throat cut. The Reverend Mr. Ezekiel Black, a part-time Methodist minister and an itinerant US Marshall is called in. This original western mystery was inspired by the great Sherlock Holmes classic, *A Study in Scarlet.*

The Brand of the Flying Four. This case all began one quiet evening in a room in Kansas City. A few weeks later, a gruesome murder, took place in Denver. By the time Rev. Black had solved the mystery, justice, of the frontier variety, not the courtroom, had been meted out. The story is inspired by *The Sign of the Four* by Arthur Conan Doyle, and like that story, it combines murder most foul, and romance most enticing.

Collection Sets for eBooks and paperback are available at *40% off the price of buying them separately.*

Collection One

The Sign of the Third

The Hudson Valley Mystery

A Case of Identity Theft

The Bald-Headed Trust

Studying Scarlet

The Mystery of the Five Oranges

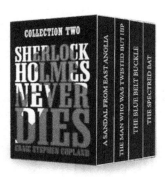

Collection Two

A Sandal from East Anglia

The Man Who Was Twisted
But Hip

The Blue Belt Buckle

The Spectred Bat

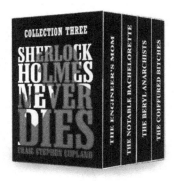

Collection Three

The Engineer's Mom

The Notable Bachelorette

The Beryl Anarchists

The Coiffured Bitches

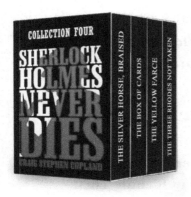

Collection Four

The Silver Horse, Braised

The Box of Cards

The Yellow Farce

The Three Rhodes Not Taken

Collection Five

The Stock Market Murders

The Glorious Yacht

The Most Grave Ritual

The Spy Gate Liars

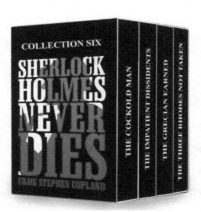

Collection Six

The Cuckold Man

The Impatient Dissidents

The Grecian, Earned

The Three Rhodes Not
    Taken

The Naval Treaty:

The Original Sherlock Holmes Story

Arthur Conan Doyle

The Naval Treaty

The July which immediately succeeded my marriage was made memorable by three cases of interest, in which I had the privilege of being associated with Sherlock Holmes and of studying his methods. I find them recorded in my notes under the headings of "The Adventure of the Second Stain," "The Adventure of the Naval Treaty," and "The Adventure of the Tired Captain." The first of these, however, deals with interest of such importance and implicates so many of the first families in the kingdom that for many years it will be impossible to make it public. No case, however, in which Holmes was engaged has ever illustrated the value of his analytical methods so clearly or has impressed those who were associated with him so deeply. I still retain an almost verbatim report of the interview in which he demonstrated the true facts of the case to Monsieur Dubugue of the Paris police, and Fritz von Waldbaum, the well-known specialist of Dantzig, both of whom had wasted their energies upon what proved to be side-issues. The new century will have come, however, before the story can be safely told. Meanwhile I pass on to the second on my list, which promised also at one time to be of national importance, and was marked by several incidents which give it a quite unique character.

During my school-days I had been intimately associated with a lad named Percy Phelps, who was of much the same age as myself, though he was two classes ahead of me. He was a very brilliant boy, and carried away every prize which the school had to offer, finished his exploits by winning a scholarship which sent him on to continue his triumphant career at Cambridge. He was, I remember, extremely well connected, and even when we were all little boys together we knew that his mother's brother was Lord Holdhurst, the great conservative politician. This gaudy relationship did him little good at school. On the contrary, it seemed rather a piquant thing to us to chevy him about the playground and hit him over the shins with a wicket. But it was another thing when he came out into the world. I heard vaguely that his abilities and the influences which he commanded had won him a good position at the Foreign Office, and then he passed completely out of my mind until the following letter recalled his existence:

Briarbrae, Woking.

My dear Watson,—I have no doubt that you can remember "Tadpole" Phelps, who was in the fifth form when you were in the third. It is possible even that you may have heard that through my uncle's influence I obtained a good appointment at the Foreign Office, and that I was in a situation of trust and honor until a horrible misfortune came suddenly to blast my career.

There is no use writing of the details of that dreadful event. In the event of your acceding to my request it is probable that I shall have to narrate them to you. I have only just recovered from nine weeks of brain-fever, and am still exceedingly weak. Do you think that you could bring your friend Mr. Holmes down to see me? I should like to have his opinion of the case, though the authorities assure me that nothing more can be done. Do try to bring him down, and as soon as possible. Every minute seems an hour while I live in this state of horrible suspense. Assure him that if I have not asked his advice sooner it was not because I did not appreciate his talents, but because I have been off my head ever since the blow fell. Now I am clear again, though I dare not think of it too much for fear of a relapse. I am still so weak that I have to write, as you see, by dictating. Do try to bring him.

Your old school-fellow,
Percy Phelps.

There was something that touched me as I read this letter, something pitiable in the reiterated appeals to bring Holmes. So moved was I that even had it been a difficult matter I should have tried it, but of course I knew well that Holmes loved his art, so that he was ever as ready to bring his aid as his client could be to receive it. My wife agreed with me that not a moment should be lost in laying the matter before him, and so within an hour of breakfast-time I found myself back once more in the old rooms in Baker Street.

Holmes was seated at his side-table clad in his dressing-gown, and working hard over a chemical investigation. A large curved retort was boiling furiously in the bluish flame of a Bunsen burner, and the distilled drops were condensing into a two-litre measure. My friend hardly glanced up as I entered, and I, seeing that his investigation must be of importance, seated myself in an arm-chair and waited. He dipped into this bottle or that, drawing out a few drops of each with his glass pipette, and finally brought a test-tube containing a solution over to the table. In his right hand he held a slip of litmus-paper.

"You come at a crisis, Watson," said he. "If this paper remains blue, all is well. If it turns red, it means a man's life." He dipped it into the test-tube and it flushed at once into a dull, dirty crimson. "Hum! I thought as much!" he cried. "I will be at your service in an instant, Watson. You will find tobacco in the Persian slipper." He turned to his desk and scribbled off several telegrams, which were handed over to the page-boy. Then he threw himself down into the chair opposite, and drew up his knees until his fingers clasped round his long, thin shins.

"A very commonplace little murder," said he. "You've got something better, I fancy. You are the stormy petrel of crime, Watson. What is it?"

I handed him the letter, which he read with the most concentrated attention.

"It does not tell us very much, does it?" he remarked, as he handed it back to me.

"Hardly anything."

"And yet the writing is of interest."

"But the writing is not his own."

"Precisely. It is a woman's."

"A man's surely," I cried.

"No, a woman's, and a woman of rare character. You see, at the commencement of an investigation it is something to know that your client is in close contact with someone who, for good or evil, has an exceptional nature. My interest is already awakened in the case. If you are ready we will start at once for Woking, and see this diplomatist who is in such evil case, and the lady to whom he dictates his letters."

We were fortunate enough to catch an early train at Waterloo, and in a little under an hour we found ourselves among the fir-woods and the heather of Woking. Briarbrae proved to be a large detached house standing in extensive grounds within a few minutes' walk of the station. On sending in our cards we were shown into an elegantly appointed drawing-room, where we were joined in a few minutes by a rather stout man who received us with much hospitality. His age may have been nearer forty than thirty, but his cheeks were so ruddy and his eyes so merry that he still conveyed the impression of a plump and mischievous boy.

"I am so glad that you have come," said he, shaking our hands with effusion. "Percy has been inquiring for you all morning. Ah, poor old chap, he clings to any straw! His father and his mother asked me to see you, for the mere mention of the subject is very painful to them."

"We have had no details yet," observed Holmes. "I perceive that you are not yourself a member of the family."

Our acquaintance looked surprised, and then, glancing down, he began to laugh.

"Of course you saw the J H monogram on my locket," said he. "For a moment I thought you had done something clever. Joseph Harrison is my name, and as Percy is to marry my sister Annie I shall at least be a relation by marriage. You will find my sister in his room, for she has nursed him hand-and-foot this two months back. Perhaps we'd better go in at once, for I know how impatient he is."

The chamber in which we were shown was on the same floor as the drawing-room. It was furnished partly as a sitting and partly as a bedroom, with flowers arranged daintily in every nook and corner. A young man, very pale and worn, was lying upon a sofa near the open window, through which came the rich scent of the garden and the balmy summer air. A woman was sitting beside him, who rose as we entered.

"Shall I leave, Percy?" she asked.

He clutched her hand to detain her. "How are you, Watson?" said he, cordially. "I should never have known you under that moustache, and I dare say you would not be prepared to swear to me. This I presume is your celebrated friend, Mr. Sherlock Holmes?"

I introduced him in a few words, and we both sat down. The stout young man had left us, but his sister still remained with her hand in that of the invalid. She was a striking-looking woman, a little short and thick for symmetry, but with a beautiful olive complexion, large, dark, Italian eyes, and a wealth of deep black hair. Her rich tints made the white face of her companion the more worn and haggard by the contrast.

"I won't waste your time," said he, raising himself upon the sofa. "I'll plunge into the matter without further preamble. I was a happy and successful man, Mr. Holmes, and on the eve of being married, when a sudden and dreadful misfortune wrecked all my prospects in life.

"I was, as Watson may have told you, in the Foreign Office, and through the influences of my uncle, Lord Holdhurst, I rose rapidly to a responsible position. When my uncle became foreign minister in this administration he gave me several missions of trust, and as I always brought them to a successful conclusion, he came at last to have the utmost confidence in my ability and tact.

"Nearly ten weeks ago—to be more accurate, on the 23d of May—he called me into his private room, and, after complimenting me on the good work which I had done, he informed me that he had a new commission of trust for me to execute.

"'This,' said he, taking a gray roll of paper from his bureau, 'is the original of that secret treaty between England and Italy of which, I regret to say, some rumors have already got into the public press. It is of enormous importance that nothing further should leak out. The French or the Russian embassy would pay an immense sum to learn the contents of these papers. They should not leave my bureau were it not that it is absolutely necessary to have them copied. You have a desk in your office?'

"'Yes, sir.'

"'Then take the treaty and lock it up there. I shall give directions that you may remain behind when the others go, so that you may copy it at your leisure without fear of being overlooked. When you have finished, relock both the original and the draft in the desk, and hand them over to me personally to-morrow morning.'

"I took the papers and—"

"Excuse me an instant," said Holmes. "Were you alone during this conversation?"

"Absolutely."

"In a large room?"

"Thirty feet each way."

"In the centre?"

"Yes, about it."

"And speaking low?"

"My uncle's voice is always remarkably low. I hardly spoke at all."

"Thank you," said Holmes, shutting his eyes; "pray go on."

"I did exactly what he indicated, and waited until the other clerks had departed. One of them in my room, Charles Gorot, had some arrears of work to make up, so I left him there and went out to dine. When I returned he was gone. I was anxious to hurry my work, for I knew that Joseph—the Mr. Harrison whom you saw just now—was in town, and that he would travel down to Woking by the eleven-o'clock train, and I wanted if possible to catch it.

"When I came to examine the treaty, I saw at once that it was of such importance that my uncle had been guilty of no exaggeration in what he had said. Without going into details, I may say that it defined the position of Great Britain towards the Triple Alliance, and fore-shadowed the policy which this country would pursue in the event of the French fleet gaining a complete ascendancy over that of Italy in the Mediterranean. The questions treated in it were purely naval. At the end were the signatures of the high dignitaries who had signed it. I glanced my eyes over it, and then settled down to my task of copying.

"It was a long document, written in the French language, and containing twenty-six separate articles. I copied as quickly as I could, but at nine o'clock I had only done nine articles, and it seemed hopeless for me to attempt to catch my train. I was feeling drowsy and stupid, partly from my dinner and also from the effects of a long day's work. A cup of coffee would clear my brain. A commissionnaire remains all night in a little lodge at the foot of the stairs, and is in the habit of making coffee at his spirit-lamp for any of the officials who may be working overtime. I rang the bell, therefore, to summon him.

"To my surprise, it was a woman who answered the summons, a large, coarse-faced, elderly woman, in an apron. She explained that she was the commissionnaire's wife, who did the charing, and I gave her the order for the coffee.

"I wrote two more articles and then, feeling more drowsy than ever, I rose and walked up and down the room to stretch my legs. My coffee had not yet come, and I wondered what the cause of the delay could be. Opening the door, I started down the corridor to find out. There was a straight passage, dimly lighted, which led from the room in which I had been working, and was the only exit from it. It ended in a curving staircase, with the commissionnaire's lodge in the passage at the bottom. Half way down this staircase is a small landing, with another passage running into it at right angles. This second one leads by means of a second small stair to a side door, used by servants, and also as a short cut by clerks when coming from Charles Street. Here is a rough chart of the place."

"Thank you. I think that I quite follow you," said Sherlock Holmes.

"It is of the utmost importance that you should notice this point. I went down the stairs and into the hall, where I found the commissionnaire fast asleep in his box, with the kettle boiling furiously upon the spirit-lamp. I took off the kettle and blew out the lamp, for the water was spurting over the floor. Then I put out my hand and was about to shake the man, who was still sleeping soundly, when a bell over his head rang loudly, and he woke with a start.

"'Mr. Phelps, sir!' said he, looking at me in bewilderment.

"'I came down to see if my coffee was ready.'

"'I was boiling the kettle when I fell asleep, sir.' He looked at me and then up at the still quivering bell with an ever-growing astonishment upon his face.

"'If you was here, sir, then who rang the bell?' he asked.

"'The bell!' I cried. 'What bell is it?'

"'It's the bell of the room you were working in.'

"A cold hand seemed to close round my heart. Someone, then, was in that room where my precious treaty lay upon the table. I ran frantically up the stair and along the passage. There was no one in the corridors, Mr. Holmes. There was no one in the room. All was exactly as I left it, save only that the papers which had been committed to my care had been taken from the desk on which they lay. The copy was there, and the original was gone."

Holmes sat up in his chair and rubbed his hands. I could see that the problem was entirely to his heart. "Pray, what did you do then?" he murmured.

"I recognized in an instant that the thief must have come up the stairs from the side door. Of course I must have met him if he had come the other way."

"You were satisfied that he could not have been concealed in the room all the time, or in the corridor which you have just described as dimly lighted?"

"It is absolutely impossible. A rat could not conceal himself either in the room or the corridor. There is no cover at all."

"Thank you. Pray proceed."

"The commissionnaire, seeing by my pale face that something was to be feared, had followed me upstairs. Now we both rushed along the corridor and down the steep steps which led to Charles Street. The door at the bottom was closed, but unlocked. We flung it open and rushed out. I can distinctly remember that as we did so there came three chimes from a neighboring clock. It was quarter to ten."

"That is of enormous importance," said Holmes, making a note upon his shirt-cuff.

"The night was very dark, and a thin, warm rain was falling. There was no one in Charles Street, but a great traffic was going on, as usual, in Whitehall, at the extremity. We rushed along the pavement, bare-headed as we were, and at the far corner we found a policeman standing.

"'A robbery has been committed,' I gasped. 'A document of immense value has been stolen from the Foreign Office. Has anyone passed this way?'

"'I have been standing here for a quarter of an hour, sir,' said he; 'only one person has passed during that time—a woman, tall and elderly, with a Paisley shawl.'

"'Ah, that is only my wife,' cried the commissionnaire; 'has no one else passed?'

"'No one.'

"'Then it must be the other way that the thief took,' cried the fellow, tugging at my sleeve.

"'But I was not satisfied, and the attempts which he made to draw me away increased my suspicions.

"'Which way did the woman go?' I cried.

"'I don't know, sir. I noticed her pass, but I had no special reason for watching her. She seemed to be in a hurry.'

"'How long ago was it?'

"'Oh, not very many minutes.'

"'Within the last five?'

"'Well, it could not be more than five.'

"'You're only wasting your time, sir, and every minute now is of importance,' cried the commissionnaire; 'take my word for it that my old woman has nothing to do with it, and come down to the other end of the street. Well, if you won't, I will.' And with that he rushed off in the other direction.

"But I was after him in an instant and caught him by the sleeve.

"'Where do you live?' said I.

"'16 Ivy Lane, Brixton,' he answered. 'But don't let yourself be drawn away upon a false scent, Mr. Phelps. Come to the other end of the street and let us see if we can hear of anything.'

"Nothing was to be lost by following his advice. With the policeman we both hurried down, but only to find the street full of traffic, many people coming and going, but all only too eager to get to a place of safety upon so wet a night. There was no lounger who could tell us who had passed.

"Then we returned to the office, and searched the stairs and the passage without result. The corridor which led to the room was laid down with a kind of creamy linoleum which shows an impression very easily. We examined it very carefully, but found no outline of any footmark."

"Had it been raining all evening?"

"Since about seven."

"How is it, then, that the woman who came into the room about nine left no traces with her muddy boots?"

"I am glad you raised the point. It occurred to me at the time. The charwomen are in the habit of taking off their boots at the commissionnaire's office, and putting on list slippers."

"That is very clear. There were no marks, then, though the night was a wet one? The chain of events is certainly one of extraordinary interest. What did you do next?

"We examined the room also. There is no possibility of a secret door, and the windows are quite thirty feet from the ground. Both of them were fastened on the inside. The carpet prevents any possibility of a trap-door, and the ceiling is of the ordinary whitewashed kind. I will pledge my life that whoever stole my papers could only have come through the door."

"How about the fireplace?"

"They use none. There is a stove. The bell-rope hangs from the wire just to the right of my desk. Whoever rang it must have come right up to the desk to do it. But why should any criminal wish to ring the bell? It is a most insoluble mystery."

"Certainly the incident was unusual. What were your next steps? You examined the room, I presume, to see if the intruder had left any traces—any cigar-end or dropped glove or hairpin or other trifle?"

"There was nothing of the sort."

"No smell?"

"Well, we never thought of that."

"Ah, a scent of tobacco would have been worth a great deal to us in such an investigation."

"I never smoke myself, so I think I should have observed it if there had been any smell of tobacco. There was absolutely no clue of any kind. The only tangible fact was that the commissionnaire's wife—Mrs. Tangey was the name—had hurried out of the place. He could give no explanation save that it was about the time when the woman always went home. The policeman and I agreed that our best plan would be to seize the woman before she could get rid of the papers, presuming that she had them.

"The alarm had reached Scotland Yard by this time, and Mr. Forbes, the detective, came round at once and took up the case with a great deal of energy. We hired a hansom, and in half an hour we were at the address which had been given to us. A young woman opened the door, who proved to be Mrs. Tangey's eldest daughter. Her mother had not come back yet, and we were shown into the front room to wait.

"About ten minutes later a knock came at the door, and here we made the one serious mistake for which I blame myself. Instead of opening the door ourselves, we allowed the girl to do so. We heard her say, 'Mother, there are two men in the house waiting to see you,' and an instant afterwards we heard the patter of feet rushing down the passage. Forbes flung open the door, and we both ran into the back room or kitchen, but the woman had got there before us. She stared at us with defiant eyes, and then, suddenly recognizing me, an expression of absolute astonishment came over her face.

"'Why, if it isn't Mr. Phelps, of the office!' she cried.

"'Come, come, who did you think we were when you ran away from us?' asked my companion.

"'I thought you were the brokers,' said she, 'we have had some trouble with a tradesman.'

"'That's not quite good enough,' answered Forbes. 'We have reason to believe that you have taken a paper of importance from the Foreign Office, and that you ran in here to dispose of it. You must come back with us to Scotland Yard to be searched.'

"It was in vain that she protested and resisted. A four-wheeler was brought, and we all three drove back in it. We had first made an examination of the kitchen, and especially of the kitchen fire, to see whether she might have made away with the papers during the instant that she was alone. There were no signs, however, of any ashes or scraps. When we reached Scotland Yard she was handed over at once to the female searcher. I waited in an agony of suspense until she came back with her report. There were no signs of the papers.

"Then for the first time the horror of my situation came in its full force. Hitherto I had been acting, and action had numbed thought. I had been so confident of regaining the treaty at once that I had not dared to think of what would be the consequence if I failed to do so. But now there was nothing more to be done, and I had leisure to realize my position. It was horrible. Watson there would tell you that I was a nervous, sensitive boy at school. It is my nature. I thought of my uncle and of his colleagues in the Cabinet, of the shame which I had brought upon him, upon myself, upon every one connected with me. What though I was the victim of an extraordinary accident? No allowance is made for accidents where diplomatic interests are at stake. I was ruined, shamefully, hopelessly ruined. I don't know what I did. I fancy I must have made a scene. I have a dim recollection of a group of officials who crowded round me, endeavoring to soothe me. One of them drove down with me to Waterloo, and saw me into the Woking train. I believe that he would have come all the way had it not been that Dr. Ferrier, who lives near me, was going down by that very train. The doctor most kindly took charge of me, and it was well he did so, for I had a fit in the station, and before we reached home I was practically a raving maniac.

"You can imagine the state of things here when they were roused from their beds by the doctor's ringing and found me in this condition. Poor Annie here and my mother were broken-hearted. Dr. Ferrier had just heard enough from the detective at the station to be able to give an idea of what had happened, and his story did not mend matters. It was evident to all that I was in for a long illness, so Joseph was bundled out of this cheery bedroom, and it was turned into a sick-room for me. Here I have lain, Mr. Holmes, for over nine weeks, unconscious, and raving with brain-fever. If it had not been for Miss Harrison here and for the doctor's care I should not be speaking to you now. She has nursed me by day and a hired nurse has looked after me by night, for in my mad fits I was capable of anything. Slowly my reason has cleared, but it is only during the last three days that my memory has quite returned. Sometimes I wish that it never had. The first thing that I did was to wire to Mr. Forbes, who had the case in hand. He came out, and assures me that, though everything has been done, no trace of a clue has been discovered. The commissionnaire and his wife have been examined in every way without any light being thrown upon the matter. The suspicions of the police then rested upon young Gorot, who, as you may remember, stayed over time in the office that night. His remaining behind and his French name were really the only two points which could suggest suspicion; but, as a matter of fact, I did not begin work until he had gone, and his people are of Huguenot extraction, but as English in sympathy and tradition as you and I are. Nothing was found to implicate him in any way, and there the matter dropped. I turn to you, Mr. Holmes, as absolutely my last hope. If you fail me, then my honor as well as my position are forever forfeited."

The invalid sank back upon his cushions, tired out by this long recital, while his nurse poured him out a glass of some stimulating medicine. Holmes sat silently, with his head thrown back and his eyes closed, in an attitude which might seem listless to a stranger, but which I knew betokened the most intense self-absorption.

"Your statement has been so explicit," said he at last, "that you have really left me very few questions to ask. There is one of the very utmost importance, however. Did you tell anyone that you had this special task to perform?"

"No one."

"Not Miss Harrison here, for example?"

"No. I had not been back to Woking between getting the order and executing the commission."

"And none of your people had by chance been to see you?"

"None."

"Did any of them know their way about in the office?"

"Oh, yes, all of them had been shown over it."

"Still, of course, if you said nothing to anyone about the treaty these inquiries are irrelevant."

"I said nothing."

"Do you know anything of the commissionnaire?"

"Nothing except that he is an old soldier."

"What regiment?"

"Oh, I have heard—Coldstream Guards."

"Thank you. I have no doubt I can get details from Forbes. The authorities are excellent at amassing facts, though they do not always use them to advantage. What a lovely thing a rose is!"

He walked past the couch to the open window, and held up the drooping stalk of a moss-rose, looking down at the dainty blend of crimson and green. It was a new phase of his character to me, for I had never before seen him show any keen interest in natural objects.

"There is nothing in which deduction is so necessary as in religion," said he, leaning with his back against the shutters. "It can be built up as an exact science by the reasoner. Our highest assurance of the goodness of Providence seems to me to rest in the flowers. All other things, our powers our desires, our food, are all really necessary for our existence in the first instance. But this rose is an extra. Its smell and its color are an embellishment of life, not a condition of it. It is only goodness which gives extras, and so I say again that we have much to hope from the flowers."

Percy Phelps and his nurse looked at Holmes during this demonstration with surprise and a good deal of disappointment written upon their faces. He had fallen into a reverie, with the moss-rose between his fingers. It had lasted some minutes before the young lady broke in upon it.

"Do you see any prospect of solving this mystery, Mr. Holmes?" she asked, with a touch of asperity in her voice.

"Oh, the mystery!" he answered, coming back with a start to the realities of life. "Well, it would be absurd to deny that the case is a very abstruse and complicated one, but I can promise you that I will look into the matter and let you know any points which may strike me."

"Do you see any clue?"

"You have furnished me with seven, but, of course, I must test them before I can pronounce upon their value."

"You suspect some one?"

"I suspect myself."

"What!"

"Of coming to conclusions too rapidly."

"Then go to London and test your conclusions."

"Your advice is very excellent, Miss Harrison," said Holmes, rising. "I think, Watson, we cannot do better. Do not allow yourself to indulge in false hopes, Mr. Phelps. The affair is a very tangled one."

"I shall be in a fever until I see you again," cried the diplomatist.

"Well, I'll come out by the same train to-morrow, though it's more than likely that my report will be a negative one."

"God bless you for promising to come," cried our client. "It gives me fresh life to know that something is being done. By the way, I have had a letter from Lord Holdhurst."

"Ha! What did he say?"

"He was cold, but not harsh. I dare say my severe illness prevented him from being that. He repeated that the matter was of the utmost importance, and added that no steps would be taken about my future—by which he means, of course, my dismissal—until my health was restored and I had an opportunity of repairing my misfortune."

"Well, that was reasonable and considerate," said Holmes. "Come, Watson, for we have a good day's work before us in town."

Mr. Joseph Harrison drove us down to the station, and we were soon whirling up in a Portsmouth train. Holmes was sunk in profound thought, and hardly opened his mouth until we had passed Clapham Junction.

"It's a very cheery thing to come into London by any of these lines which run high, and allow you to look down upon the houses like this."

I thought he was joking, for the view was sordid enough, but he soon explained himself.

"Look at those big, isolated clumps of building rising up above the slates, like brick islands in a lead-colored sea."

"The board-schools."

"Light-houses, my boy! Beacons of the future! Capsules with hundreds of bright little seeds in each, out of which will spring the wise, better England of the future. I suppose that man Phelps does not drink?"

"I should not think so."

"Nor should I, but we are bound to take every possibility into account. The poor devil has certainly got himself into very deep water, and it's a question whether we shall ever be able to get him ashore. What did you think of Miss Harrison?"

"A girl of strong character."

"Yes, but she is a good sort, or I am mistaken. She and

her brother are the only children of an iron-master somewhere up Northumberland way. He got engaged to her when traveling last winter, and she came down to be introduced to his people, with her brother as escort. Then came the smash, and she stayed on to nurse her lover, while brother Joseph, finding himself pretty snug, stayed on too. I've been making a few independent inquiries, you see. But to-day must be a day of inquiries."

"My practice—" I began.

"Oh, if you find your own cases more interesting than mine—" said Holmes, with some asperity.

"I was going to say that my practice could get along very well for a day or two, since it is the slackest time in the year."

"Excellent," said he, recovering his good-humor. "Then we'll look into this matter together. I think that we should begin by seeing Forbes. He can probably tell us all the details we want until we know from what side the case is to be approached."

"You said you had a clue?"

"Well, we have several, but we can only test their value by further inquiry. The most difficult crime to track is the one which is purposeless. Now this is not purposeless. Who is it who profits by it? There is the French ambassador, there is the Russian, there is whoever might sell it to either of these, and there is Lord Holdhurst."

"Lord Holdhurst!"

"Well, it is just conceivable that a statesman might find himself in a position where he was not sorry to have such a document accidentally destroyed."

"Not a statesman with the honorable record of Lord Holdhurst?"

"It is a possibility and we cannot afford to disregard it. We shall see the noble lord to-day and find out if he can tell us anything. Meanwhile I have already set inquiries on foot."

"Already?"

"Yes, I sent wires from Woking station to every evening paper in London. This advertisement will appear in each of them."

He handed over a sheet torn from a note-book. On it was scribbled in pencil: "L10 reward. The number of the cab which dropped a fare at or about the door of the Foreign Office in Charles Street at quarter to ten in the evening of May 23d. Apply 221 B, Baker Street."

"You are confident that the thief came in a cab?"

"If not, there is no harm done. But if Mr. Phelps is correct in stating that there is no hiding-place either in the room or the corridors, then the person must have come from outside. If he came from outside on so wet a night, and yet left no trace of damp upon the linoleum, which was examined within a few minutes of his passing, then it is exceeding probable that he came in a cab. Yes, I think that we may safely deduce a cab."

"It sounds plausible."

"That is one of the clues of which I spoke. It may lead us to something. And then, of course, there is the bell—which is the most distinctive feature of the case. Why should the bell ring? Was it the thief who did it out of bravado? Or was it someone who was with the thief who did it in order to prevent the crime? Or was it an accident? Or was it—?" He sank back into the state of intense and silent thought from which he had emerged; but it seemed to me, accustomed as I was to his every mood, that some new possibility had dawned suddenly upon him.

It was twenty past three when we reached our terminus, and after a hasty luncheon at the buffet we pushed on at once to Scotland Yard. Holmes had already wired to Forbes, and we found him waiting to receive us—a small, foxy man with a sharp but by no means amiable expression. He was decidedly frigid in his manner to us, especially when he heard the errand upon which we had come.

"I've heard of your methods before now, Mr. Holmes," said he, tartly. "You are ready enough to use all the information that the police can lay at your disposal, and then you try to finish the case yourself and bring discredit on them."

"On the contrary," said Holmes, "out of my last fifty-three cases my name has only appeared in four, and the police have had all the credit in forty-nine. I don't blame you for not knowing this, for you are young and inexperienced, but if you wish to get on in your new duties you will work with me and not against me."

"I'd be very glad of a hint or two," said the detective, changing his manner. "I've certainly had no credit from the case so far."

"What steps have you taken?"

"Tangey, the commissionnaire, has been shadowed. He left the Guards with a good character and we can find nothing against him. His wife is a bad lot, though. I fancy she knows more about this than appears."

"Have you shadowed her?"

"We have set one of our women on to her. Mrs. Tangey drinks, and our woman has been with her twice when she was well on, but she could get nothing out of her."

"I understand that they have had brokers in the house?"

"Yes, but they were paid off."

"Where did the money come from?"

"That was all right. His pension was due. They have not shown any sign of being in funds."

"What explanation did she give of having answered the bell when Mr. Phelps rang for the coffee?"

"She said that he husband was very tired and she wished to relieve him."

"Well, certainly that would agree with his being found a little later asleep in his chair. There is nothing against them then but the woman's character. Did you ask her why she hurried away that night? Her haste attracted the attention of the police constable."

"She was later than usual and wanted to get home."

"Did you point out to her that you and Mr. Phelps, who started at least twenty minutes after her, got home before her?"

"She explains that by the difference between a 'bus and a hansom."

"Did she make it clear why, on reaching her house, she ran into the back kitchen?"

"Because she had the money there with which to pay off the brokers."

"She has at least an answer for everything. Did you ask her whether in leaving she met anyone or saw any one loitering about Charles Street?"

"She saw no one but the constable."

"Well, you seem to have cross-examined her pretty thoroughly. What else have you done?"

"The clerk Gorot has been shadowed all these nine weeks, but without result. We can show nothing against him."

"Anything else?"

"Well, we have nothing else to go upon—no evidence of any kind."

"Have you formed a theory about how that bell rang?"

"Well, I must confess that it beats me. It was a cool hand, whoever it was, to go and give the alarm like that."

"Yes, it was queer thing to do. Many thanks to you for what you have told me. If I can put the man into your hands you shall hear from me. Come along, Watson."

"Where are we going to now?" I asked, as we left the office.

"We are now going to interview Lord Holdhurst, the cabinet minister and future premier of England."

We were fortunate in finding that Lord Holdhurst was still in his chambers in Downing Street, and on Holmes sending in his card we were instantly shown up. The statesman received us with that old-fashioned courtesy for which he is remarkable, and seated us on the two luxuriant lounges on either side of the fireplace. Standing on the rug between us, with his slight, tall figure, his sharp features, thoughtful face, and curling hair prematurely tinged with gray, he seemed to represent that not too common type, a nobleman who is in truth noble.

"Your name is very familiar to me, Mr. Holmes," said he, smiling. "And, of course, I cannot pretend to be ignorant of the object of your visit. There has only been one occurrence in these offices which could call for your attention. In whose interest are you acting, may I ask?"

"In that of Mr. Percy Phelps," answered Holmes.

"Ah, my unfortunate nephew! You can understand that

our kinship makes it the more impossible for me to screen him in any way. I fear that the incident must have a very prejudicial effect upon his career."

"But if the document is found?"

"Ah, that, of course, would be different."

"I had one or two questions which I wished to ask you, Lord Holdhurst."

"I shall be happy to give you any information in my power."

"Was it in this room that you gave your instructions as to the copying of the document?"

"It was."

"Then you could hardly have been overheard?"

"It is out of the question."

"Did you ever mention to any one that it was your intention to give any one the treaty to be copied?"

"Never."

"You are certain of that?"

"Absolutely."

"Well, since you never said so, and Mr. Phelps never said so, and nobody else knew anything of the matter, then the thief's presence in the room was purely accidental. He saw his chance and he took it."

The statesman smiled. "You take me out of my province there," said he.

Holmes considered for a moment. "There is another very important point which I wish to discuss with you," said he. "You feared, as I understand, that very grave results might follow from the details of this treaty becoming known."

A shadow passed over the expressive face of the statesman. "Very grave results indeed."

"Any have they occurred?"

"Not yet."

"If the treaty had reached, let us say, the French or Russian Foreign Office, you would expect to hear of it?"

"I should," said Lord Holdhurst, with a wry face.

"Since nearly ten weeks have elapsed, then, and nothing has been heard, it is not unfair to suppose that for some reason the treaty has not reached them."

Lord Holdhurst shrugged his shoulders.

"We can hardly suppose, Mr. Holmes, that the thief took the treaty in order to frame it and hang it up."

"Perhaps he is waiting for a better price."

"If he waits a little longer he will get no price at all. The treaty will cease to be secret in a few months."

"That is most important," said Holmes. "Of course, it is a possible supposition that the thief has had a sudden illness—"

"An attack of brain-fever, for example?" asked the statesman, flashing a swift glance at him.

"I did not say so," said Holmes, imperturbably. "And now, Lord Holdhurst, we have already taken up too much of your valuable time, and we shall wish you good-day."

"Every success to your investigation, be the criminal who it may," answered the nobleman, as he bowed us out the door.

"He's a fine fellow," said Holmes, as we came out into Whitehall. "But he has a struggle to keep up his position. He is far from rich and has many calls. You noticed, of course, that his boots had been resoled. Now, Watson, I won't detain you from your legitimate work any longer. I shall do nothing more to-day, unless I have an answer to my cab advertisement. But I should be extremely obliged to you if you would come down with me to Woking to-morrow, by the same train which we took yesterday."

I met him accordingly next morning and we traveled down to Woking together. He had had no answer to his advertisement, he said, and no fresh light had been thrown upon the case. He had, when he so willed it, the utter immobility of countenance of a red Indian, and I could not gather from his appearance whether he was satisfied or not with the position of the case. His conversation, I remember, was about the Bertillon system of measurements, and he expressed his enthusiastic admiration of the French savant.

We found our client still under the charge of his devoted nurse, but looking considerably better than before. He rose from the sofa and greeted us without difficulty when we entered.

"Any news?" he asked, eagerly.

"My report, as I expected, is a negative one," said Holmes. "I have seen Forbes, and I have seen your uncle, and I have set one or two trains of inquiry upon foot which may lead to something."

"You have not lost heart, then?"

"By no means."

"God bless you for saying that!" cried Miss Harrison. "If we keep our courage and our patience the truth must come out."

"We have more to tell you than you have for us," said Phelps, reseating himself upon the couch.

"I hoped you might have something."

"Yes, we have had an adventure during the night, and one which might have proved to be a serious one." His expression grew very grave as he spoke, and a look of something akin to fear sprang up in his eyes. "Do you know," said he, "that I begin to believe that I am the unconscious centre of some monstrous conspiracy, and that my life is aimed at as well as my honor?"

"Ah!" cried Holmes.

"It sounds incredible, for I have not, as far as I know, an enemy in the world. Yet from last night's experience I can come to no other conclusion."

"Pray let me hear it."

"You must know that last night was the very first night

167

that I have ever slept without a nurse in the room. I was so much better that I thought I could dispense with one. I had a night-light burning, however. Well, about two in the morning I had sunk into a light sleep when I was suddenly aroused by a slight noise. It was like the sound which a mouse makes when it is gnawing a plank, and I lay listening to it for some time under the impression that it must come from that cause. Then it grew louder, and suddenly there came from the window a sharp metallic snick. I sat up in amazement. There could be no doubt what the sounds were now. The first ones had been caused by someone forcing an instrument through the slit between the sashes, and the second by the catch being pressed back.

"There was a pause then for about ten minutes, as if the person were waiting to see whether the noise had awakened me. Then I heard a gentle creaking as the window was very slowly opened. I could stand it no longer, for my nerves are not what they used to be. I sprang out of bed and flung open the shutters. A man was crouching at the window. I could see little of him, for he was gone like a flash. He was wrapped in some sort of cloak which came across the lower part of his face. One thing only I am sure of, and that is that he had some weapon in his hand. It looked to me like a long knife. I distinctly saw the gleam of it as he turned to run."

"This is most interesting," said Holmes. "Pray what did you do then?"

"I should have followed him through the open window if I

had been stronger. As it was, I rang the bell and roused the house. It took me some little time, for the bell rings in the kitchen and the servants all sleep upstairs. I shouted, however, and that brought Joseph down, and he roused the others. Joseph and the groom found marks on the bed outside the window, but the weather has been so dry lately that they found it hopeless to follow the trail across the grass. There's a place, however, on the wooden fence which skirts the road which shows signs, they tell me, as if someone had got over, and had snapped the top of the rail in doing so. I have said nothing to the local police yet, for I thought I had best have your opinion first."

This tale of our client's appeared to have an extraordinary effect upon Sherlock Holmes. He rose from his chair and paced about the room in uncontrollable excitement.

"Misfortunes never come single," said Phelps, smiling, though it was evident that his adventure had somewhat shaken him.

"You have certainly had your share," said Holmes. "Do you think you could walk round the house with me?"

"Oh, yes, I should like a little sunshine. Joseph will come, too."

"And I also," said Miss Harrison.

"I am afraid not," said Holmes, shaking his head. "I think I must ask you to remain sitting exactly where you are."

The young lady resumed her seat with an air of

displeasure. Her brother, however, had joined us and we set off all four together. We passed round the lawn to the outside of the young diplomatist's window. There were, as he had said, marks upon the bed, but they were hopelessly blurred and vague. Holmes stopped over them for an instant, and then rose shrugging his shoulders.

"I don't think anyone could make much of this," said he. "Let us go round the house and see why this particular room was chosen by the burglar. I should have thought those larger windows of the drawing-room and dining-room would have had more attractions for him."

"They are more visible from the road," suggested Mr. Joseph Harrison.

"Ah, yes, of course. There is a door here which he might have attempted. What is it for?"

"It is the side entrance for trades-people. Of course it is locked at night."

"Have you ever had an alarm like this before?"

"Never," said our client.

"Do you keep plate in the house, or anything to attract burglars?"

"Nothing of value."

Holmes strolled round the house with his hands in his pockets and a negligent air which was unusual with him.

"By the way," said he to Joseph Harrison, "you found some place, I understand, where the fellow scaled the fence.

Let us have a look at that!"

The plump young man led us to a spot where the top of one of the wooden rails had been cracked. A small fragment of the wood was hanging down. Holmes pulled it off and examined it critically.

"Do you think that was done last night? It looks rather old, does it not?"

"Well, possibly so."

"There are no marks of any one jumping down upon the other side. No, I fancy we shall get no help here. Let us go back to the bedroom and talk the matter over."

Percy Phelps was walking very slowly, leaning upon the arm of his future brother-in-law. Holmes walked swiftly across the lawn, and we were at the open window of the bedroom long before the others came up.

"Miss Harrison," said Holmes, speaking with the utmost intensity of manner, "you must stay where you are all day. Let nothing prevent you from staying where you are all day. It is of the utmost importance."

"Certainly, if you wish it, Mr. Holmes," said the girl in astonishment.

"When you go to bed lock the door of this room on the outside and keep the key. Promise to do this."

"But Percy?"

"He will come to London with us."

"And am I to remain here?"

"It is for his sake. You can serve him. Quick! Promise!"

She gave a quick nod of assent just as the other two came up.

"Why do you sit moping there, Annie?" cried her brother. "Come out into the sunshine!"

"No, thank you, Joseph. I have a slight headache and this room is deliciously cool and soothing."

"What do you propose now, Mr. Holmes?" asked our client.

"Well, in investigating this minor affair we must not lose sight of our main inquiry. It would be a very great help to me if you would come up to London with us."

"At once?"

"Well, as soon as you conveniently can. Say in an hour."

"I feel quite strong enough, if I can really be of any help."

"The greatest possible."

"Perhaps you would like me to stay there to-night?"

"I was just going to propose it."

"Then, if my friend of the night comes to revisit me, he will find the bird flown. We are all in your hands, Mr. Holmes, and you must tell us exactly what you would like done. Perhaps you would prefer that Joseph came with us so as to look after me?"

"Oh, no; my friend Watson is a medical man, you know, and he'll look after you. We'll have our lunch here, if you will permit us, and then we shall all three set off for town together."

It was arranged as he suggested, though Miss Harrison excused herself from leaving the bedroom, in accordance with Holmes's suggestion. What the object of my friend's manoeuvres was I could not conceive, unless it were to keep the lady away from Phelps, who, rejoiced by his returning health and by the prospect of action, lunched with us in the dining-room. Holmes had a still more startling surprise for us, however, for, after accompanying us down to the station and seeing us into our carriage, he calmly announced that he had no intention of leaving Woking.

"There are one or two small points which I should desire to clear up before I go," said he. "Your absence, Mr. Phelps, will in some ways rather assist me. Watson, when you reach London you would oblige me by driving at once to Baker Street with our friend here, and remaining with him until I see you again. It is fortunate that you are old school-fellows, as you must have much to talk over. Mr. Phelps can have the spare bedroom to-night, and I will be with you in time for breakfast, for there is a train which will take me into Waterloo at eight."

"But how about our investigation in London?" asked Phelps, ruefully.

"We can do that to-morrow. I think that just at present I can be of more immediate use here."
"You might tell them at Briarbrae that I hope to be back to-

morrow night," cried Phelps, as we began to move from the platform.

"I hardly expect to go back to Briarbrae," answered Holmes, and waved his hand to us cheerily as we shot out from the station.

Phelps and I talked it over on our journey, but neither of us could devise a satisfactory reason for this new development.

"I suppose he wants to find out some clue as to the burglary last night, if a burglar it was. For myself, I don't believe it was an ordinary thief."

"What is your own idea, then?"

"Upon my word, you may put it down to my weak nerves or not, but I believe there is some deep political intrigue going on around me, and that for some reason that passes my understanding my life is aimed at by the conspirators. It sounds high-flown and absurd, but consider the facts! Why should a thief try to break in at a bedroom window, where there could be no hope of any plunder, and why should he come with a long knife in his hand?"

"You are sure it was not a house-breaker's jimmy?"

"Oh, no, it was a knife. I saw the flash of the blade quite distinctly."

"But why on earth should you be pursued with such animosity?"

"Ah, that is the question."

"Well, if Holmes takes the same view, that would account for his action, would it not? Presuming that your theory is correct, if he can lay his hands upon the man who threatened you last night he will have gone a long way towards finding who took the naval treaty. It is absurd to suppose that you have two enemies, one of whom robs you, while the other threatens your life."

"But Holmes said that he was not going to Briarbrae."

"I have known him for some time," said I, "but I never knew him do anything yet without a very good reason," and with that our conversation drifted off on to other topics.

But it was a weary day for me. Phelps was still weak after his long illness, and his misfortune made him querulous and nervous. In vain I endeavored to interest him in Afghanistan, in India, in social questions, in anything which might take his mind out of the groove. He would always come back to his lost treaty, wondering, guessing, speculating, as to what Holmes was doing, what steps Lord Holdhurst was taking, what news we should have in the morning. As the evening wore on his excitement became quite painful.

"You have implicit faith in Holmes?" he asked.

"I have seen him do some remarkable things."

"But he never brought light into anything quite so dark as this?"

"Oh, yes; I have known him solve questions which presented fewer clues than yours."

"But not where such large interests are at stake?"

"I don't know that. To my certain knowledge he has acted on behalf of three of the reigning houses of Europe in very vital matters."

"But you know him well, Watson. He is such an inscrutable fellow that I never quite know what to make of him. Do you think he is hopeful? Do you think he expects to make a success of it?"

"He has said nothing."

"That is a bad sign."

"On the contrary, I have noticed that when he is off the trail he generally says so. It is when he is on a scent, and is not quite absolutely sure yet that it is the right one, that he is most taciturn. Now, my dear fellow, we can't help matters by making ourselves nervous about them, so let me implore you to go to bed and so be fresh for whatever may await us to-morrow."

I was able at last to persuade my companion to take my advice, though I knew from his excited manner that there was not much hope of sleep for him. Indeed, his mood was infectious, for I lay tossing half the night myself, brooding over this strange problem, and inventing a hundred theories, each of which was more impossible than the last. Why had Holmes remained at Woking? Why had he asked Miss Harrison to remain in the sick-room all day? Why had he been so careful not to inform the people at Briarbrae that he intended to remain near them? I cudgelled my brains until I fell asleep in the endeavor to find some explanation which would cover all these facts.

It was seven o'clock when I awoke, and I set off at once for Phelps's room, to find him haggard and spent after a sleepless night. His first question was whether Holmes had arrived yet.

"He'll be here when he promised," said I, "and not an instant sooner or later."

And my words were true, for shortly after eight a hansom dashed up to the door and our friend got out of it. Standing in the window we saw that his left hand was swathed in a bandage and that his face was very grim and pale. He entered the house, but it was some little time before he came upstairs.

"He looks like a beaten man," cried Phelps.

I was forced to confess that he was right. "After all," said I, "the clue of the matter lies probably here in town."

Phelps gave a groan.

"I don't know how it is," said he, "but I had hoped for so much from his return. But surely his hand was not tied up like that yesterday. What can be the matter?"

"You are not wounded, Holmes?" I asked, as my friend entered the room.

"Tut, it is only a scratch through my own clumsiness," he answered, nodding his good-mornings to us. "This case of yours, Mr. Phelps, is certainly one of the darkest which I have ever investigated."

"I feared that you would find it beyond you."

"It has been a most remarkable experience."

"That bandage tells of adventures," said I. "Won't you tell us what has happened?"

"After breakfast, my dear Watson. Remember that I have breathed thirty miles of Surrey air this morning. I suppose that there has been no answer from my cabman advertisement? Well, well, we cannot expect to score every time."

The table was all laid, and just as I was about to ring Mrs. Hudson entered with the tea and coffee. A few minutes later she brought in three covers, and we all drew up to the table, Holmes ravenous, I curious, and Phelps in the gloomiest state of depression.

"Mrs. Hudson has risen to the occasion," said Holmes, uncovering a dish of curried chicken. "Her cuisine is a little limited, but she has as good an idea of breakfast as a Scotch-woman. What have you here, Watson?"

"Ham and eggs," I answered.

"Good! What are you going to take, Mr. Phelps—curried fowl or eggs, or will you help yourself?"

"Thank you. I can eat nothing," said Phelps.

"Oh, come! Try the dish before you."

"Thank you, I would really rather not."

"Well, then," said Holmes, with a mischievous twinkle, "I suppose that you have no objection to helping me?"

Phelps raised the cover, and as he did so he uttered a scream, and sat there staring with a face as white as the plate upon which he looked. Across the centre of it was lying a little cylinder of blue-gray paper. He caught it up, devoured it with his eyes, and then danced madly about the room, pressing it to his bosom and shrieking out in his delight. Then he fell back into an arm-chair so limp and exhausted with his own emotions that we had to pour brandy down his throat to keep him from fainting.

"There! there!" said Holmes, soothing, patting him upon the shoulder. "It was too bad to spring it on you like this, but Watson here will tell you that I never can resist a touch of the dramatic."

Phelps seized his hand and kissed it. "God bless you!" he cried. "You have saved my honor."

"Well, my own was at stake, you know," said Holmes. "I assure you it is just as hateful to me to fail in a case as it can be to you to blunder over a commission."

Phelps thrust away the precious document into the innermost pocket of his coat.

"I have not the heart to interrupt your breakfast any further, and yet I am dying to know how you got it and where it was."

Sherlock Holmes swallowed a cup of coffee, and turned his attention to the ham and eggs. Then he rose, lit his pipe, and settled himself down into his chair.

"I'll tell you what I did first, and how I came to do it afterwards," said he. "After leaving you at the station I went for a charming walk through some admirable Surrey scenery to a pretty little village called Ripley, where I had my tea at an inn, and took the precaution of filling my flask and of putting a paper of sandwiches in my pocket. There I remained until evening, when I set off for Woking again, and found myself in the high-road outside Briarbrae just after sunset.

"Well, I waited until the road was clear—it is never a very frequented one at any time, I fancy—and then I clambered over the fence into the grounds."

"Surely the gate was open!" ejaculated Phelps.

"Yes, but I have a peculiar taste in these matters. I chose the place where the three fir-trees stand, and behind their screen I got over without the least chance of any one in the house being able to see me. I crouched down among the bushes on the other side, and crawled from one to the other—witness the disreputable state of my trouser knees—until I had reached the clump of rhododendrons just opposite to your bedroom window. There I squatted down and awaited developments.

"The blind was not down in your room, and I could see Miss Harrison sitting there reading by the table. It was quarter-past ten when she closed her book, fastened the shutters, and retired.

"I heard her shut the door, and felt quite sure that she had turned the key in the lock."

"The key!" ejaculated Phelps.

"Yes; I had given Miss Harrison instructions to lock the door on the outside and take the key with her when she went to bed. She carried out every one of my injunctions to the letter, and certainly without her cooperation you would not have that paper in your coat-pocket. She departed then and the lights went out, and I was left squatting in the rhododendron-bush.

"The night was fine, but still it was a very weary vigil. Of course it has the sort of excitement about it that the sportsman feels when he lies beside the water-course and waits for the big game. It was very long, though—almost as long, Watson, as when you and I waited in that deadly room when we looked into the little problem of the Speckled Band. There was a church-clock down at Woking which struck the quarters, and I thought more than once that it had stopped. At last however about two in the morning, I suddenly heard the gentle sound of a bolt being pushed back and the creaking of a key. A moment later the servants' door was opened, and Mr. Joseph Harrison stepped out into the moonlight."

"Joseph!" ejaculated Phelps.

"He was bare-headed, but he had a black coat thrown

over his shoulder so that he could conceal his face in an instant if there were any alarm. He walked on tiptoe under the shadow of the wall, and when he reached the window he worked a long-bladed knife through the sash and pushed back the catch. Then he flung open the window, and putting his knife through the crack in the shutters, he thrust the bar up and swung them open.

"From where I lay I had a perfect view of the inside of the room and of every one of his movements. He lit the two candles which stood upon the mantelpiece, and then he proceeded to turn back the corner of the carpet in the neighborhood of the door. Presently he stopped and picked out a square piece of board, such as is usually left to enable plumbers to get at the joints of the gas-pipes. This one covered, as a matter of fact, the T joint which gives off the pipe which supplies the kitchen underneath. Out of this hiding-place he drew that little cylinder of paper, pushed down the board, rearranged the carpet, blew out the candles, and walked straight into my arms as I stood waiting for him outside the window.

"Well, he has rather more viciousness than I gave him credit for, has Master Joseph. He flew at me with his knife, and I had to grasp him twice, and got a cut over the knuckles, before I had the upper hand of him. He looked murder out of the only eye he could see with when we had finished, but he listened to reason and gave up the papers. Having got them I let my man go, but I wired full particulars to Forbes this morning. If he is quick enough to catch his bird, well and good. But if, as I shrewdly suspect, he finds the nest empty before he gets there, why, all the better for the government. I fancy that Lord Holdhurst for one, and Mr. Percy Phelps for another, would very much rather that the affair never got as far as a police-court.

"My God!" gasped our client. "Do you tell me that during these long ten weeks of agony the stolen papers were within the very room with me all the time?"

"So it was."

"And Joseph! Joseph a villain and a thief!"

"Hum! I am afraid Joseph's character is a rather deeper and more dangerous one than one might judge from his appearance. From what I have heard from him this morning, I gather that he has lost heavily in dabbling with stocks, and that he is ready to do anything on earth to better his fortunes. Being an absolutely selfish man, when a chance presented itself he did not allow either his sister's happiness or your reputation to hold his hand."

Percy Phelps sank back in his chair. "My head whirls," said he. "Your words have dazed me."

"The principal difficulty in your case," remarked Holmes, in his didactic fashion, "lay in the fact of there being too much evidence. What was vital was overlaid and hidden by what was irrelevant. Of all the facts which were presented to us we had to pick just those which we deemed to be essential, and then piece them together in their order, so as to reconstruct this very remarkable chain of events. I had already begun to suspect Joseph, from the fact that you had intended to travel home with him that night, and that therefore it was a likely enough thing that he should call for you, knowing the Foreign Office well, upon his way. When I heard that someone had been so anxious to get into the bedroom, in which no one but Joseph could have concealed anything—you told us in your narrative how you had turned Joseph out when you arrived with the doctor—my suspicions all changed to certainties, especially as the attempt was made on the first night upon which the nurse was absent, showing that the intruder was well acquainted with the ways of the house."

"How blind I have been!"

"The facts of the case, as far as I have worked them out, are these: this Joseph Harrison entered the office through the Charles Street door, and knowing his way he walked straight into your room the instant after you left it. Finding no one there he promptly rang the bell, and at the instant that he did so his eyes caught the paper upon the table. A glance showed him that chance had put in his way a State document of immense value, and in an instant he had thrust it into his pocket and was gone. A few minutes elapsed, as you remember, before the sleepy commissionnaire drew your attention to the bell, and those were just enough to give the thief time to make his escape.

"He made his way to Woking by the first train, and

having examined his booty and assured himself that it really was of immense value, he had concealed it in what he thought was a very safe place, with the intention of taking it out again in a day or two, and carrying it to the French embassy, or wherever he thought that a long price was to be had. Then came your sudden return. He, without a moment's warning, was bundled out of his room, and from that time onward there were always at least two of you there to prevent him from regaining his treasure. The situation to him must have been a maddening one. But at last he thought he saw his chance. He tried to steal in, but was baffled by your wakefulness. You remember that you did not take your usual draught that night."

"I remember."

"I fancy that he had taken steps to make that draught efficacious, and that he quite relied upon your being unconscious. Of course, I understood that he would repeat the attempt whenever it could be done with safety. Your leaving the room gave him the chance he wanted. I kept Miss Harrison in it all day so that he might not anticipate us. Then, having given him the idea that the coast was clear, I kept guard as I have described. I already knew that the papers were probably in the room, but I had no desire to rip up all the planking and skirting in search of them. I let him take them, therefore, from the hiding-place, and so saved myself an infinity of trouble. Is there any other point which I can make clear?"

"Why did he try the window on the first occasion," I asked, "when he might have entered by the door?"

"In reaching the door he would have to pass seven bedrooms. On the other hand, he could get out on to the lawn with ease. Anything else?"

"You do not think," asked Phelps, "that he had any murderous intention? The knife was only meant as a tool."

"It may be so," answered Holmes, shrugging his shoulders. "I can only say for certain that Mr. Joseph Harrison is a gentleman to whose mercy I should be extremely unwilling to trust."

33743733R00116

Made in the USA
Middletown, DE
17 January 2019